To:

From Boy to Man

A Beautiful Butterfly

STAY Transforming

Coach Hartman

4/2014

FROM BOY TO MAN

A CONCRETE JUNGLE STORY

Tyrone Hartman, MHS, LCADC

Walk Into Your Destiny
MEDIA

ISBN: 978-0-9799641-1-4

Published by: Walk into Your Destiny, New Jersey

Book cover designed by: Walk Into Your Destiny

Printed in the United States of America

To all the boys that dare to be men

Contents

Introduction

In this book, my life's story of a troubled inner-city boy from Newark, N.J, to becoming a man with constructive principles, deep determination and an attitude fit for winners, is to inspire you. My purpose for writing this book is to be an additional resource for those who desire that light within to shine and keep burning. Part one & two in the book will start the flames, and Part three will keep the fire going. I hope you will be able to witness my personal faith, passion, motivation and determination to be great. I then ask you for a chance to assist in your journey to be great. Remember fellows, great, not regular.

My efforts put into this book are for the purpose of being a positive example and a role model. My voice speaks through the pages with care, concern, consistency, and years experience as a counselor. My life's story of struggle and courage, along with the words of motivation that follow in Part 3 were written as if I was your personal motivational coach. I have great passion as a change agent to assist others in their journey towards becoming their best-self. That's a mission I've been on for years.

You will read in the book how I admired the strength and style of a gentleman named Mr. Shaheed at a time when I was gaining self-discovery. Through identifying with him, I began to see myself as a strong man. I became someone with a vision and the power to imagine being a great man. The imagination is our land of opportunity to envision what we want our lives to look like. So go ahead, visualize and believe in the extraordinary person that's unfolding today and everyday. Family, your powers of motivation and faith will then need to play a major role in that unfolding story.

Street knowledge is a **power within** that I've gained through my life's journey. You will read my many experiences in the concrete jungle that has developed that sixth sense. The combination of street knowledge and the high level of motivation to become a successful and positive leader, there was no limit. Over the years I've become a polished professional, but my street intelligence is what has kept me indestructible. You will read about how the two fed off of each other for the benefit of personal development. The strengths I've gotten from enduring the storms of the street life have made it hard to break me down or destroy my spirit. So I look forward to sharing a story and book that can cause you to think, laugh, feel, and become more inspired to live the life you deserve.

My professional counseling background provided me with the hands-on experience of assisting others in changing their lives. In Part three of the book, you will experience words of motivation that I've share with others for many years throughout my career. Now it's time to go public. I have been employed within the mental health, substance abuse, and criminal justice environments for approximately 15 years. My job of inspiring and steering others in the right path has not been an easy task, but it has been rewarding. To feel the motivation and spirits lift in people when they are at a low point in their lives, gives me great pleasure.

There is a tone of humor in the book that allows the therapeutic experience to be more receptive by the readers.

Many times I have been called a comedian when I give lectures. Sometimes I don't know whether I should take that as a compliment or not. But it's usually to express the message was well received. My goal for this book was to create a comfortable space for you to zone in on your quest to become a more successful and happy person. I look forward to being a part of your support system.

Part One

In the City of Newark

I was born in Newark, New Jersey on October 28, 1973. My history with the street life began around the Hawthorne Avenue area from 1985 to 1997. I lived with my mother, father, sister, and two brothers. We didn't have much money, which created a strong desire for things and possessions. Financially, my parents did their best, but it wasn't enough to save me from the enemy of my inner self.

My first encounter with my materialistic side was at the age of 14, when I was in the 8th grade at Bergen Street Elementary School. I was hanging in a staircase with three boys when I pulled out a square piece of foil filled with cocaine. I said, "Look, this stuff is going to get me all the Air Jordan sneakers, Guess jeans, and nice shirts I want." At that moment I was on my way to succumbing to the images of fancy clothes and worldly desires. Education was secondary and I was then blinded by materialism.

Growing up in Newark on Hawthorne Avenue, between Clinton Place and Bergen Street, I learned something you can't buy in a soda can: "Street knowledge". I entered the life of crime at 14-years-old and at 15, I received the name that I'm still called at times, Mutah (Moo-tah). I can still clearly remember when an older brother named Rashiek said, "You look like your name should be Mutah." It's funny because that's not the most unique way to obtain a name, but it gave me a new identity, and I felt cool.

As a youth, I wasn't a big bad wolf; however, I did run with a pack. I could have easily chosen to be a gun-toting wolf or have gotten involved with many different extremely negative activities. I dedicated myself to being the local drug dealer. However, the poor environment controlling me also controlled the others around me. Poverty, disadvantaged schools, a lack of positive role models, and many false hopes were pulling all of our strings.

My development on those streets seemed like an advanced course in college. It matured me, gave me strength, and taught me ways to gain money. There was no room for slow learners; they learned early that the streets weren't a good option. Whether they constantly got arrested, shot and beaten by foes, or became drug abusers. They came to understand how slim their chances were. They were weak. As for me, I had all the right characteristics for the fate that was to come. I was a fast learner, popular with the girls, and guys with ruthless reputations.

The inner city's so-called glamorous life, led to my aspirations to become a big-time drug dealer. Now, Hawthorne Avenue was a place where young people from the surrounding areas came to hang out at the Boys and Girls Club, eat at Bragman's Deli, play basketball, or ride up and down in their cars on the long strip. I was a part of the Hawthorne Avenue Crew (H.A.C.). We made sure we were always freshly dressed in the latest fashions, but we all could fight with our fists (and had to prove it). I was also exposed to the high rollers from Avon Avenue, Chancellor Avenue, Bergen Street, the Prince Street Posse (P.S.P.), Hayes Homes Projects, and some parts of Irvington and East Orange. The slang, Goose Bombers coats, Shell Toe Adidas, big "dookie" gold chains, three-finger rings, the N.Y. styled blowout Afros, cars with the booming systems, and the fan club of girls, all came nicely packaged within my four-block radius community.

It may be hard to believe that there were no positive influences or role models that swayed me from getting knee-deep in the street life. While there were some influences, I was uninterested in any wake up calls. Images of honest, working people, or Boys and Girls Club counselors did not move me. I remember when unmarked vans would pull up to the sidewalk, and men would jump out and chase us through the streets and backyards. I later learned that this scary ordeal involved men from the Nation of Islam. It was their method of trying to force "knowledge of self" upon us. They knew we were untrained soldiers, in a struggle we couldn't even comprehend. Too bad we had absolutely no idea.

My older brother Ali-Red was known for his fighting skills. He was known as "Ali-Boom Bap" because of his one-two punch. He was a roughneck, and maintained street credibility. No one could approach the Hawthorne Avenue posse with any drama, without having to face Ali-Red. People used to exclaim, "Ali-Red is your brother?!" I heard this so much that I became afraid of him.

My brother and his crew took care of the beefs (disagreements or problems) on the streets. Their clique consisted of my brother, Tink and Taheem. Tink, the pretty boy, was known for fast punching and kicking. Tink was like our own Run from Run-DMC, as he brought bling and style to our block. Taheem never lost a fight. If you were to imagine Mike Tyson growing up on the Newark streets, Taheem would personify this vision. We called him "Booty Chin" because he had a deep dimple in his chin that girls found attractive, and because he could fight, he was more of a don with the opposite sex. My brother had other affiliates but these were the main three that were known for causing havoc. And the more they terrorized people, the more street credibility I gained. My brother is still alive, but Tink and Taheem were both violently killed before they were 30-years-old.

A Drug Dealer's Dream

By age15, I was certified as being a member of the Hawthorne Avenue Crew, complete with fringe benefits. I wore this badge of honor, foolishly parading around as if we owned that street. Inner city street hustlers usually have no clue or forget that the local and federal government ultimately ruled their neighborhoods. And all of us were clueless. It was my block; and I was passionate, serious, dedicated, loyal, and infatuated with it. School became unimportant, and the few family rules and curfews were also irrelevant. The "My Block" concept gave me superficial power, yet blinded my ability to envision a promising future. When it came to looking towards the future, the 1st and the 15th of every month were all that mattered. On those days the welfare checks and food stamps allowed the local drug addicts to buy their poison from me. It was as if I took an oath, "By the power invested in thee, I pronounce your marriage to the Block." And what a challenging marriage it was. I had the courage to take on dangers that could have killed men. In the big scope of things, I was a child in a drug-infested area, who according to statistics will be dead before the age of 25.

We abided by The Crack Commandments, which required us to look out for the cops; identify escape routes; watch out for potential robbers; keep our eyes on drugs stashed away; never get high off your supply; never keep the drugs in your house; create code names for the police; never keep too much money on you; no lay-a-way plans for addicts; have better products than competitors; and of course, there were a host of other rules.

In addition to being a money-hungry man, I had to master

techniques to maintain my reputation. Slang became a second language; my unique dialect was like a survival tool. For instance, if someone yelled in a crowd, "See him" or "Go up top", it meant someone was about to fight. Which led to another prerequisite: fighting. Being good wasn't enough; I had to know how to defend myself against two people at the same time, just in case. Next was adhering to the dress code, which determined what people thought of you. If you had on a corny outfit, people laughed at you in your face. I never had that problem. And the important art of manipulation was key to my survival. If I didn't know how to sway people toward my ideas, I would have fallen prey to the schemers, weaklings and wild boys. Besides, I never wanted to be a follower. So with all that knowledge, who needed college when Psychology, slang as a second language, and skills of group dynamics were all taught in the streets? And I thought I was the master of these arts, when in reality I had so much more to learn.

Music to the Ears

When I was 16, Hip Hop was strictly our music, as mainstream America turned up its nose and refused to embrace an artist like KRS-One, whose lyrics I worshipped. KRS-One rhymed so you could understand every concept, and was skilled and animated enough to capture New York street life on a cassette tape. In the hit song, "Are you a Philosopher," he said, *"You got to have style / and learn to be original /* or *everybody's gonna wanna diss you."* He earned the title "The Teacher".

Listening to A Tribe Called Quest awakened my sense of Black pride. I was so unaware of racial dynamics in America. (Imagine that!) Q-Tip and the gang exposed me to culture, which began filling a serious void within me. They were a part of the Native Tongue, a group that consisted of The Jungle Brothers, Queen Latifah, DJ Red Alert and De La Soul. These ambassadors of Hip-Hop were truly inspiring. And Leaders of the New School with Busta Rhymes made me happy, carefree, and youthful, which were vital emotions growing up in the inner city. I made it my business to see the majority of them perform. Of course, I could afford orchestra seats, due to my hustling revenue.

So in 1991 at the Apollo Theater in Harlem, I witnessed KRS-One, A Tribe Called Quest, and Leaders of the New School give a performance that has remained one of the shining moments of my urban youth experience. When I saw A Tribe Called Quest and Leaders of the New School perform their infamous, "What's the Scenario" song, I actually shed a tear. It was euphoric and dreamlike. The Apollo was the vessel that materialized my culture, through entertainers I could relate to, right in front of my eyes. This historical theater brought heaven to the 'hood.

The X Clan, whose mantra, "The red, the black, and the green," reflected a poetic but aggressive manner I didn't encounter on Hawthorne Avenue. Their confidence and militancy turned a page in my life's book. I began wearing black beads and Doctor Martin boots, just like them. I didn't know what the beads meant, but it felt good to be different and I wasn't clowned for wearing my Black Panther-gear on the Avenue either. Everyone knew I had enough money to buy anything I wanted. That phase didn't last too long, but it lent some diversity to my stylish aura. The only comment a person would say was, "Mutah, you're buggin'," but they knew I kept my street hustler's swagger up at all times. And as for Hip Hop music, it helped me get through my hard knock life on the streets, and that's why I will always have a reverence for it.

Thug Gentleman

In 1991, I was selling $1,500 worth of cocaine a day. I was inducted into the Hall of Young-and-'Hood-Rich Fame. Even amongst the old people, they expressed that I would have easily progressed well in the work force. I was a natural leader. My hustle was sharp, as I had tried my best to emulate older hustlers, who motivated me with their cars. Fendi-styled jeeps, Nissans with spoiler kits dropped low, top of the line music systems, Corvettes, and luxury Cadillacs made my spirit excited to get to their level.

Everyone was so busy mastering the rules of hustling that no never showed envy for the money I made. In my 'hood we held the view that there was enough of the pie to go around. If someone from the block fell off their road to riches, they would turn ten dollars into one thousand dollars in one day, by staying out past midnight hustling. The money would be made even if the weather temperature was a blistering 20 degrees. The hunger for money would numb the body and spirit to any and all of the abuse on the streets.

As I ascended through the ranks, I made plans to buy a hooptie or an old used car. Why not have tangible and visible assets? One day I was standing on the corner of Hawthorne Avenue and Wolcott Terrace with about $2,500 in my pocket. I was trying to decide which car lot I should go to, when a guy from Avon Ave drove up in the newest Mazda RX-7 *with* a spoiler kit. It was 1991 and this car was pretty hot in the 'hood. This fellow, also known as a young thorough drug dealer, made my hooptie purchase plans vanish. I knew I could eventually buy a stylish car, so instead of buying a waste of a car, I went downtown Newark and bought some fresh gear and an extra-large gold nugget bracelet that covered my entire wrist. It got me lots of attention, and in my state of mind, this investment was a great decision. Today, I truly understand that I was only feeding a superficial ego. There was so much KRS-One could teach me.

Club Sensations was a well-known Hip-Hop venue that hosted popular entertainers such as Big Daddy Kane, Rakim, Biz Markie, and other artists. It's where I could show off my ill-gotten gains—jewelry and clothes. I really thought I was somebody when I got in the club without proper identification. Based on the company I kept, the club's security guards respected me. And my image, I made sure it was, as we said back then, fly. I had a fresh Afro haircut, leather Starter Jacket, a big gold chain hanging around my neck, and a gold bracelet on my wrist. As I stood in line, I got a lot of attention because the older guys would yell out, "Yo, Mutah, where are you?" "Make sure nobody goes in, if he doesn't get in," "Yo, make sure nobody tries to start any stuff with him." Even the girls used to whisper, "There's Mutah."

Inside the club we were a loud bunch, walking around the club, taking group pictures, socializing with other guys, grabbing girls' arms for attention, and at times fighting. This atmosphere reinforced my need to make more money, just so I could be more stylish *next* week at the club, which is where I got a heavy dose of Hip Hop each time. I had so much fun watching the baggy-jean dancers battled it out on the floor. In many ways, Club Sensations was a break from the streets, but it didn't pull me away far enough.

Eventually I began to supply dealers with wholesale cocaine prices. They didn't have to go to New York City anymore, as I was a local resource. I recruited others to hustle for me and I watched the money come in even faster. I had a new and improved status, but I stayed focused on acquiring my next asset—a hot ride. There were many cars that the boys in the 'hood drove, but the rule was that the ride should fit one's style. Plus, once the word got out that you purchased a car, you automatically gained respect of being a true hustler.

Young and Flashy

My first car was a burgundy 1990 Mazda RX-7 with five-speed gears, and the first thing I did was ride up Hawthorne Avenue, a long hill, to show the 'hood my new toy. My comrades were happy because my new purchase motivated them to also scheme for more cash in the streets. Girls were really impressed because I already had a reputation for wearing nice clothes and now, here I was at 16 years old with a flashy car. One of my hustling associates, Kevin from 12th street and Avon, told me that I should immediately put the car in the shop for a make over. I took his suggestion and v*oila!* My car had a spoiler all around the body, a spoiler wing, and chrome rims. It was unbelievable. I couldn't believe I was its proud owner. Months later, however, I bought an even more expensive car. Boy was I living it up, foolishly in the ghetto!

My friend, Money Spencer, from Lyons Avenue was incarcerated when he decided to sell his black convertible Mazda RX-7. I had the money—$10,000—to buy it, and before I knew it, I was one of the first dudes to sport a convertible. To top it off, an associate from Clinton Place, took me to a shop where I purchased chrome BBS rims with new tires. I paid $2,400 for tires, which complimented the equally pricey rims. To a concrete jungle king like me, it was heaven.

One week after I had the car, I took a late-night ride to Boston Fried Chicken on Elizabeth Avenue. I ordered my food and as I got back into my car, someone came behind me with a gun. I immediately turned around with my hands up and saw that the weapon was pointed toward my stomach. After the attacker went into my pockets and took my money, he snatched the car keys from my hands. "Move away from the car, now," he said. At that moment, I looked him in the eyes and I saw fear, it was the perfect opportunity to throw in a fast punch, which knocked him unconscious.

The gun fell to the ground and he fell inside of the car by the gas pedal. I quickly pulled both of his legs out of the car, but he woke up and soon we were fighting for the gun. He got it back, but I fought and wrestled with him so much that he fired the gun at me and ran. This was an event that could have ended in a deadly way. Days later, everyone had heard that I was almost carjacked. Another one of my associates, named Mufi from Irving Turner Boulevard, found out who the predator was and gave him some physical damage.

On my 17th birthday, I spent the day at a car dealership in Millburn, NJ. I was there to buy a 1993 (even though it was 1992) Mazda MX-6 with an older woman, who agreed to purchase the car in her name. I had never bought a car from a showroom, so this was a grand new experience. I took my BBS rims from the convertible and put them on the new car, added a spoiler wing, and tinted the windows. I was paid, living amid poverty, while purchasing cars left and right. This was the hottest car I had ever bought, and soon it would be my last big splurge for a long time.

"Hey Mutah, let's get something to eat," said Ali-Red, hustling for me at the time. I used to take him and my other hustlers to Red Lobster for lunch almost daily. We'd jump in my car, blasting the rap group Onyx, and be thrilled at everyone looking at the car from behind those tinted windows. I felt like a young prince.

The Big Bang

But this was only the beginning of the end. Soon I began to lose money and shortly thereafter–my cool. At one time, a close accomplice stole $10,000 from me. Those that were dealing drugs for me began to cause problems by stealing, and cheating. To make up for the losses, my brother had suggested I sell wholesale marijuana, which I added to my portfolio. It was no surprise that he also took advantage of our relationship. My money evaporated even faster. I decided that I needed to cut off all the people who were hustling for me, to become a one-man show.

Soon thereafter, I was arrested. We were on Hawthorne Avenue inside Bragman's Deli, and undercover cops came in to search everyone. One guy actually had drugs on him and I had $1,500 in my pocket, which they decided to arrest me too. I guess I was the usual suspect. By this time I was 18-years-old. It would be my first time in the county jail, but a lot of people knew me and the experience was oddly like being on the streets. While I was there, I didn't reflect on gaining control of my life because I was more concerned with upholding my street image. After about two days, I posted bail and was back in the streets fully energized.

I soon set my sights on conspiring with really grimy thugs, the ones who liked to rob people. Even my mother began to notice my new affiliates, and they weren't the boyish knuckleheads she was used to seeing with me. I also began selling drug dealers larger amounts of supply, with the purpose of getting them robbed, in order to resell the goods. This was my new hustle, and with it came a lot of guilt and shame. My car now had guns on the floor, instead of new sneaker boxes. I was wobbling in my mess of criminal behaviors, because my greed within had no limits.

One day the police pulled behind me with their sirens flashing, as I parked my car on Hawthorne Avenue. Frantic and shocked, I pulled off and a high-speed chase began. The fact that I had a gun and drugs on me didn't make things better. As I was speeding through the streets, I saw people pointing at my car in surprise and I began to shed tears of disbelief—my life was in shambles. The chase finally ended in Irvington with ten police cars present when I crashed into a parked car. The air bag released and although it almost knocked me unconscious, I jumped out and tried to run before the cops caught me. I wasn't fast enough. And as the mace was sprayed in my eyes, I felt like *Native Son's* Bigger Thomas—without hope, desperate to survive, and destined for doom.

The word on the street was that I crashed my car and was arrested. I was taken to the precinct and roughed up by the police, but I was in no position to protest. My family came down to get information about my charge. My mother started screaming and crying when she saw my face, which was bloody and bruised after the air bag impact and scuffle with the cops. I shouted to her, "I'm okay Ma. Just go home and wait by the phone in case I call you." I too began to cry because I was suddenly able to connect to my mother's pain. My Titanic ship was sinking, and there was nothing I could do.

I was placed in the Essex County Jail, briefly before I was bussed to the Essex County Jail Annex in Caldwell. Being chained to another inmate in a crowded van seemed like the worst ride of my life. My stylish clothes were replaced by the jailhouse, orange "carrot" suit. That was the first time I felt powerless and afraid.

The County Jail Annex looked like a haunted house surrounded by barbed wire gates. As I entered the facility, I encountered a smell that was like nothing I ever experienced—it almost caused me to vomit. To this day, I can only describe it as a mixture of what appeared to be industrial chemicals and men who hadn't bathed in weeks. As I was stripped searched, it felt like a piece of my soul was being chipped off with every command. *Take off your clothes, wiggle your fingers, open your mouth and wiggle your tongue, rub your hands through your hair, turn around, show the bottom of feet, bend over and cough.* It was humiliating, and while it was normal practice in this institution, I never was comfortable with it. I had set my sights on a road to superficial wealth—but fate had other plans and it seemed that I had lost the fight.

I was housed in the Modules, which were trailers put together to make a small community for inmates. We slept two to a room and the doors opened and closed at certain times. Lock-in time was 10 PM and they reopened at 6 AM for breakfast. Throughout the day, a correctional officer took a count of inmates. Inmates picked up laundry, while we filled out commissary slips to order toiletries and snacks. A barber came by to give haircuts every two weeks. Whenever others from within the facility came to our housing area, we became excited and in high spirits, just at the sight of a different face. There was only one telephone and shower for a group of 20 men, who had also fallen victim to the enemy within themselves.

On Lock Down

For six months, I assimilated into the culture of incarceration; learning to laugh, joke, and adapt to the daily routine. The visits I got from friends and family, along with phone calls I made, helped me cope.

As soon as I would receive a bail for the current charge, I knew I had the money to pay it. However, there was a warrant for my arrest and no bail set. I had no idea that there was a warrant out for my arrest, especially since the courts had an alias I previously used. In fact, I thought my brother had used my name, in order to escape trouble with the law. I was confused and upset. I later found out that I had a warrant after not going to court for the arrest in the Bragman's Deli. I felt that there was no case against me because I only had money in my pocket at the time of the arrest. I remembered telling the cops that I was merely a sandwich customer, and I also told the guy I got arrested with to say he didn't know me. I was confident that I would be home soon.

Many times I was transported to the court building in Newark and stayed for hours in the holding cell without appearing in front of the judge that day. Others, who were waiting, received or gave, "bull-pin therapy". We all had problems and sought to get help from fellow inmates, even if it was just a sympathetic ear. Going back and forth to court was painful because everyday I was a fool who hoped that I would soon be released.

One day I finally saw the Judge, and was informed that my case was now headed to Superior Court instead of municipal court. I was being charged with conspiracy to selling Control Dangerous Substances (CDS). All I could think to myself was, "What happened? Where did this come from? It must be a mistake, because I didn't get arrested for selling drugs. After searching my mental database, nothing made any sense until my public defender at the time, told me the bad news. The guy that I was arrested with told the cops that he was selling drugs for me!

I learned that this guy had already signed a statement against me, and now I had to get ready for trial or either except a plea bargain. I felt like someone had just shot me, and any hopes I had of going home begun to fade out by frustration and anger.

As I road back to the County Jail Annex, I had a whirlwind of thoughts. I couldn't believe that someone from Hawthorne Avenue, "my block", that I knew for many years would turn against me for no reason. He was someone we considered to be one of the "old heads" on the block, so I definitely didn't expect him to bow down to threats from the law. My cellmate made things clear for me. "He told on you because it's going to get him less jail time if he says you conspired with him to sell drugs," he said. This made sense. I did a little investigation amongst my peers who validated my cellmate's argument. I felt so dumb because they all knew this was a known practice done by snitches. But I did feel a little relieved because now I knew what I was up against.

Betrayed and Bitter

The reality was that my situation had gotten worse. I contacted my family and updated them on my court case. They were more surprised with who betrayed me, than with the stakes being even higher for me to be released. My family asked if I was certain about my accusations of the betrayal, because I told them to let the streets know that he snitched. My mother was devastated and scared because things became more complex. Her love was expressed by minimizing her own stress, worries and financial difficulties.

My mother began to visit me more, and I cried often about living apart from her and the world I loved so much. She represented all of the important things that I missed and had taken for granted. I had just turned 18 and was the youngest child, so I was still a mama's boy. One day during a visit my mother said, "No one owes you anything and you need to let go of the feelings of that boy betraying you." I went to sleep with her advice on my mind and when I awakened the next day, I decided to take her advice. Those feelings had turned me into a bitter man, because I ended up using so much time and energy ranting about how wrong I felt I was done, when in fact I had some serious atoning to do in my own life. My mother's words of wisdom came right on time; it was necessary medicine—raw, but for the best.

I told the lawyer that I decided to hire, that I would rather go to trial instead of taking a plea. Other inmates who had similar cases and were found not guilty influenced my decision. So to trial I went, with the notion that since the cops didn't arrest me with any drugs, my release was certain. One day, my lawyer showed me the statement that implicating me in the drug deal with my peer's signature on it. My attorney wanted me to be wise in my decision to take the case to trial, but I was stubborn.

My family and friends came to the trial, which played out just like a movie. It was so surreal to me. The police officers were called in to testify against me, and I remember when the prosecutor asked one of the officers, "Do you recognize the person who conspired in the drug deal?"

The officer pointed at me and said, "Yes, that's him right there."

I felt a sharp pain in my stomach, just listening to an officer lie so easily. The next day I came back to court and they called my co-defendant to the stand.

The prosecutor asked, while pointing at me, "Do you know him and was he a drug supplier on Hawthorne Avenue? Did he conspire in your drug dealings?"

He responded, "Yes, I know him and he conspired in my drug dealings."

I heard my brother say, ", He's really snitching on Mutah."

I had a look of disbelief, because the unimaginable thought of him involving me had been actualized once he said the long awaited words. The prosecutor went on to persuade the jury that since one of my peers was testifying against me, ultimately I was in fact a villain. The verdict would be read the next day. I talked to myself all that night. Even though I was a drug supplier, this conspiracy charge was not true. But at the end of the day, I had to except all that came with the game. This was pay for all the stuff I didn't get caught doing.

What's the Verdict?

The next day I went to court to receive the verdict, and I really didn't know what was going to happen. It was like I was hit with a brick from the blind side. Boom! The jury found me guilty of conspiracy. I heard my family's shock and my mother's scream. Not knowing what to do, I just put my head between my legs. I felt so numb and I didn't know what to expect next. I wanted to throw a tantrum. I hated my lawyer. The trial was over and there was no turning back the hands of time. I was a convicted criminal. I was on the losing team and I was a certified felon faced with jail time. I was scheduled to come back to court next month for sentencing. The lawyer said that he would have all of my previous charges combined with the guilty verdict, so I could move on with my life once I finished my incarceration.

Upon returning to the County Jail Annex, everyone wanted to know what happened. "Were you found not guilty?" "Yo' Mutah, you're about to go home, right?" All I could do was shake my head, because I didn't feel like talking. I went into my cell to lay-down on the bed and fell asleep.

"Mutah get up, stop that stressing," said my cellmate. "Listen, I've been to prison before and you'll be alright. Your family will be waiting on you to come home. The streets will be the same when you come home, so it's time to focus, my brother." I listened to my cellmate because he was Muslim and we had shared the cell for months. At the time, I really didn't know what it meant to be Muslim, but I know it made him very humble. I got up out of the bed and decided I wanted to shave all of my hair off to symbolize the major changes that were about to take place. I was taking my position in the web of America's social issues and statistics of an incarcerated Black man.

The month before my sentencing, I wrote many letters and contacted everyone that I knew, in order to let them know I was found guilty. I even started going to Christian services that were held in a room with a few inmates. I was searching for something to save me from my current position of despair. The night before I went to sentencing, I prayed and sang songs to God in the facilities church. When I was a little boy, my aunt who was a pastor, owned a church where I used to go to eat lunch and dinner. This was the extent of my involvement with any religious institution. But here I was at 18, praying for my life.

My cellmate told me that if I wrote the judge a letter asking for leniency, she might lighten up the sentence. I also asked my mother to bring me some new clothes, so that I could look presentable. So with the well-written letter, nice clothes, and my prayers to Jesus, I figured everything would be just fine. I was nervous though, and I even smoked a cigarette despite being repulsed at the smell. As my former lifestyle flashed through my mind, the only thing I could say was, "Damn".

Time to Pay the Piper

The hour came and it was time. My lawyer said everything is going to be alright, which made me feel the new clothes and prayers to Jesus were working already. I went into the courtroom and the judge asked, "Is there anything that you want to say before sentencing?" Things were falling right into place, so I read my please-baby-please letter. After she said, "Thank you" and paused for a moment, she stated: "I am sentencing you to five years with a three-year stipulation. You are not eligible for parole until three years."

My first thoughts were, "That letter, or any of that other stuff, didn't work". Then I turned around and looked at my crying mother. My ego had operated to destroy me, and I had been disregarding the genuinely important things in life for many years. It was now time to pay the piper.

For the first time in my life, I took a look at my future. I was in a position where I had to examine the pain of spending thirty-six months away from the world and the people I loved. However, I was out of the street equation that caused my demise. The chapter had closed on my previous lifestyle. Did the streets abuse me or did I abuse the streets? Well first, the man makes the habit; then the habit, makes the man. So I started it, and the streets finished the story.

What was my mother going to do, now that it was certain that I wasn't coming home? Many thoughts passed through my mind. My boat had been rocked like never before. I had to be incarcerated for *three* years before parole. I felt so stupid—ashamed that I didn't have the power to stop my own train wreck.

Throughout all the trial and getting convicted, I would

soon be a father. I seriously lacked the emotional stability to handle all of these trials and tribulations in my life. A week after my sentencing, my son, Tyrone S. Hartman was born premature at 1 pound and 7 ounces. There I was, a part of the negative statistics of "babies having babies". My anxiety was at its peak due to this emotional catastrophe. How could someone in my predicament respond? The only thing I could do was cry and be thankful that he survived a very early birth. The fact that I wasn't there when he was born and couldn't visualize how he looked made it even harder for me. All I knew was that I now had a child and my present life was in ruins. I definitely knew nothing about being a father. My ship sank all at once.

Before I was sent to the final correctional facility, I found out that I was going to lose my car. The woman, who had it in her name, decided to get the car from the towing company and fix it, before moving out of state. It was her gain and my loss, which by then seemed to be a normal occurrence in my life. Being so powerless while I was incarcerated took a big chuck of my spirit. I had no skills or training to maintain my damaged self-esteem. At that point I felt like a sucker—beat down and broken.

I experienced the Trilogy from hell. I lost the trial, my son was born prematurely, and my car was gone (not that I could have driven it while I was in jail). All of these troubles made me weak emotionally, but it revealed so much to me. I looked reality in the face. I would play my position as an incarcerated Black man with low self-esteem that needed to experience a new way of life. I slowly shed my grandiose image and began to gradually develop a new way of thinking.

State Property

Finally, after my first phase of incarceration, I arrived at Mountain View Correctional Facility in Annandale, N.J. The bus filled with inmates destined to live in this new society. My stomach had butterflies as if I were going to explore a new land, except that the people occupying it were criminals. Again, I was stripped searched, which did nothing but take another piece of my self-esteem. Afterward, the correctional officers began to yell, "When I call your name, raise your hand, so I can let you know where you are going to be housed."

"A. Williams, you will be housed in Cottage 1," said the officer. A. Williams was the alias I used throughout my incarceration. So along with eight others, we were taken to Cottage [illegible] As soon as we entered, a Caucasian inmate that was also a new arrival cut his wrist. "Where is all this blood on the floor coming from," I yelled. This was before he passed out in front of me. This new land was intimidating and blood signaled danger. The guy tried to commit suicide with a piece of a razor. This was the experience that initiated me into a new lifestyle and state of mind. That was not pleasant.

The word spread that I came to the facility, mainly because I was a major player on one of the sets in Newark. "Renaissance City," as it's known by today, had a reputation for having some of the worst criminals and was revered throughout New Jersey's correctional facilities. At first, I was amazed at all of the different people from all over New Jersey, and even some from out of state. For years, I had a four-block radius mentality, which made me unfamiliar with other parts of the Garden State. Although the men in the facility were approximately 90 percent Black, I had no idea how they operated in their 'hoods. It was a culture shock. However, I did come to this facility with some skills on how to function in an incarcerated setting, but this place was much bigger than I anticipated. My first objective was to learn the routine. I knew I would appear less confused if I moved and operated accordingly.

"What's up brother?" The second Caucasian inmate I had met since arriving to the facility was down to earth, although at first I didn't think we were going to get along. He slept on the bottom of the iron bunk bed to which I was assigned. I never had a conversation or any normal interaction with a Caucasian, and now one was my bunkie. Truthfully, I didn't have any interest in knowing any of them. I wasn't influenced enough by the media to have gotten the picture that Caucasians were the Americans with big entitlement issues. I didn't get the memo.

I was a Black boy lost in the wilderness of America and didn't even know that I was classified as a minority. I had never heard of Fredrick Douglass, Huey Newton, Nat Turner, W.E.B Du Bois, Nelson Mandela or Apartheid, Langston Hughes, Al Sharpton, Medgar Evers, Brown vs. The Board Education, Dred Scott vs. Sanford, Emmett Till, Blaxploitation, The Civil Rights Movement, Black colleges, Affirmative Action, the NAACP, or anything else related to history that affected me directly. No wonder I had no real self-pride, that could have possibly help save me from self-destruction. I didn't even have in-depth knowledge of the hateful atmosphere between the races.

"What's up money? My name is Mutah and I'm from

Newark," I said.

"I'm Keith and I'm from Bloomfield." he replied.

Since I just arrived, I chose to limit my conversation. As days went by though, we began talking more and I became comfortable. He noticed that a lot of people knew me, so he decided to find out some things about my past on his own. Investigating associates while incarcerated was a normal practice, because you just never knew whom you might be dealing with. Keith's conversation focused on books and people who changed America. I didn't know most of the people he talked about, but I became interested. At times, we would talk through the night, because I was suddenly curious about American history and other cultures. My bunkie gave me the first entire book I had ever read in my life, which was the *Autobiography of Malcolm X*. Now I had heard of Malcolm X before, because he was pretty popular in my community, at least on a superficial level. At first I was intimidated by the thickness of the book, but I figured that I had *a lot* of spare time to read.

I quickly learned the daily routines because the people I knew showed me the ropes and how to move around the facility. The cottage I was housed in was two stories high with over 60 inmates. I slept on the first floor in the dormitory. I had no choice but to assimilate into my new role. The daily routine consisted of following orders from the correctional officers, no matter how you felt about the task that they assigned.

Eventually I met people from Camden and found out the city was actually worse than Newark. At the time there was a violent group in Camden named after Malcolm X. I don't know why they used his name, when they allegedly committed some of the most heinous crimes in the city. They were also known for allegedly selling a lot of drugs, which made Camden one of the most respected cities amongst the inmates.

I met guys from Paterson and quickly found out that they all thought they were good boxers. Because some very good professional boxers *were* trained in Paterson and there are a lot of boxing gyms, which gave those inmates the image they boasted about. Many of them became good friends while I was in Annandale.

The person who slept in the bunk next to mine was named B.D. and he was also from Paterson. He was the first person that insisted I listen to Biggie Smalls' music. I remember B.D. use to say, "Just listen to what he is saying." I had my own Walkman, but he would take his earphones off and put them to my ears, just so I hear Biggie. My first and only physical fight there, was actually with someone from Paterson. After the fight, we actually became good associates. I interacted with these guys from all over New Jersey, which was really my first Social Science project.

A New Path: Education

At the facility, everyone who was 21-years-old and under, had the choice of working on the grounds of the facility or attending school and vocational classes. I planned to occupy my entire day with the G.E.D. course and a vocational carpentry class. There was a small waiting list but a week later I was in. My mother always wanted me to finish high school or get, as she called it, my Good Enough Diploma (G.E.D.). I decided to take up carpentry because one day I overheard some older men talking about young boys growing up without knowing how to even hammer a nail straight. I was in classes from 8:30 AM to 4:00 PM, which was a productive way to fill up my day. After school, I would read the *Autobiography of Malcolm X.* This book helped foster the beginning of my self-revolution, and I became aware that a war existed within me. I needed an identity badly, because the only things I identified with were the fickle dreams of a drug dealer.

I excelled in both of my classes and sent my mother many things that I crafted in the vocational carpentry course. When she came to visit me, she would proudly pick up her gifts. The idea of being able to give her something of significance, gave me back some of my self-esteem. I remember asking her did anyone in our family work well with their hands because I had learned so fast. She reminded me that my father could fix and build things easily. I could see that she was happy with the way I utilized my time, and to see her pleased, was further motivation for me. During visits, my mother would tell me that I always had a good spirit and was always different from the other neighborhood boys. I listened attentively because after reading the Autobiography of Malcolm X, I really wanted to be different. My mother was there for me and on every visit she would say, "There is only one way, and that's the right way."

My mother finally got her chance to interact with me intelligently and intimately. When I was on the streets ripping and running, we didn't talk as much. As my mother's youngest child, she enjoyed seeing my inner growth and new positive behaviors.

This metamorphosis caused me to become obsessed with learning more information. As I continued in both courses, there came an opportunity to take the G.E.D. test. I prepared approximately six months until I was ready, and here was the chance. I was very focused and determined to do my best. So I took the test and had to wait on the results. Everyone who took it was full of anxiety, which was shown by constantly asking each other, "Did the results come back yet?" "How do you think you did on the test?" "Was the test hard for you?" To us all, it felt like the results took forever.

While I anxiously awaited the results, I still participated in carpentry class and began taking a life skills course. This class covered areas such as the difference between wants and needs, and how to manage money properly. When I was on the street, I had no reason to take these things into consideration. I didn't work for my money and I didn't respect the many rules that came with having that power.

Good Enough Diploma (G.E.D.)

There was also a session on relationship roles in families, which enabled me to reflect on how I was raised and some of the lacking components within my own family. I now had a son and although I was unprepared to be a father, taking the life skills course gave me some insight into living a responsible life. By the time this four-week course ended, the G.E.D. results were back. You could sense the nervousness in the air throughout the facility. In bustling groups, we rushed to the classroom on the board that listed those who had passed their exam. I squeezed my way through to the front and looked on the long printout for my name. In capital letters I saw the word, PASS. "Yes sir, I passed the first time. But what do you expect?" I instantly became full of pride, after a month of being on the edge. As I walked back through the crowd, which parted like the Red Sea, I could hear, "He passed too, let him through" being mumbled. This experience added more on to the self-esteem that I needed to restore.

After learning the good news, the first thing I did was call my mother. For me it was a big accomplishment, because it made me feel intelligent, especially since I dropped out of high school. I knew that having a high school diploma or G.E.D. was something every adult should have as a minimum asset. When I told my mother, she started to cry and shared that she believed there was a positive future ahead for me. It was my mother's hope that turned on a light switch. The idea of having a legal and productive lifestyle was a possibility for me, and I began to develop an attitude that my existence on this planet was above selling drugs or standing on a dangerous corner.

My new attitude was heavily connected to my studies in Black history while I was incarcerated. The guys from Asbury, Neptune, and Paterson introduced me to the culture of Five-Percenters. It was the first time I heard a philosophy that professed that the Black man was God. It was interesting and much of the information centered on a structured body of knowledge that was constantly analyzed during their 'ciphers'. A cipher is when a group of people stands in a circle formation, strongly expressing a topic.

The men had names like Justice-Born, Understanding, Knowledge, Divine, Supreme, and Star. I listened to them pontificate passionately about not being puppets for the Caucasian race, which they labeled as 'devils'. Even my Caucasian bunkie was fascinated with them. They called others who were in the cottage, "savages", if they behaved foolishly. These guys had standards I had never applied to myself or to my peers in the past. The premise I was most attracted to was the idea of obtaining "knowledge of self". This concept was something I read in the *Autobiography of Malcolm X*, in which Malcolm insisted was the first ingredient a Black man needed to begin a better lifestyle for himself and his family. And since Malcolm was my first positive role model, I began to attend the ciphers they had every night. My quest for knowledge was becoming more intense. However, I never committed myself to their Five-Percenter culture.

I soon entered a basic Computer Programming course with my bunkie. I had never used a computer, so it was a chance for me to learn, despite my frustration with all the technological terms. Being in the class, however, gave me a chance to interact with others from different cottages. One gentleman from Philadelphia named Abdul, began to share information about all the other positive benefits available in the facility's program. He also informed me of a radio program on New York City's Hot 97 called "Street Soldiers", which covered issues that affected the inner city community and Hip Hop. It came on every Sunday, and it was as if I had discovered social and race issues I had never before noticed. I had no idea that Black people faced intense social deprivations and challenges on a daily basis. Before long, I became known as a Street Soldier devotee, which was fine with me. The program humbled me, because I had learned more about America's great ills and power.

Abdul gave me information on how to apply for college by introducing me to Mr. Lucas, the head of the facility's educational department. Mr. Lucas was an older Black man who focused only on education. I tried to choose my words carefully when I spoke to him for the first time. He impressed me because of his respect for education, and I certainly had never met anyone like him on Hawthorne Avenue. As he spoke, I remained quiet and listened. I had recently read a book that said, "A person only knows you're a fool, when you open up your mouth with nothing to say of substance." I didn't want to fit that description. Mr. Lucas explained that since I obtained my G.E.D, I could apply to Essex County College in Newark. He also went over financial aid and government grants that were available. We didn't discuss what I wanted to study in college, which was fine because at the time, I didn't know what to choose as my major. That was a good decision to go and meet Mr. Lucas. It was simple; he was welcoming and shared priceless information with me.

I no longer indulged so much with others that I knew

from the streets, since that usually involved glamorizing the life of drug dealing and other negative risky behaviors. I was no longer interested in that kind of a high. If I wasn't in any of my classes, I was reading or studying materials or maybe working on a carpentry project. I was at the stage where I understood my inner self and I was ready to fight for a better life.

Getting to Know Me

I secluded myself so often that I became known as a humble and respected person who read many books. A few of my favorites were: *American History* by Howard Zinn; *Countering the Conspiracy to Destroy Black Boys* by Jawanza Kunjufu; *Black Skin White mask* by Frantz Fanon and *The Mis-Education of the Negro* by Carter G. Woodson. Through these works, I began obtaining "knowledge of self".

I soon met a brother named Ahid Barnes, who was also from Newark. His father was a well-known poet. I first noticed him in the 'ciphers' as someone who was very knowledgeable. We became close and found out that we knew some of the same people on the streets. It was he who let me borrow Sister Soldier's memoir, *No Disrespect.* I had never known much about her, and as I read the book I kept looking at her face on the back of the book cover. She was a fierce and intelligent woman that blew my mind! I am forever grateful for that book loan because I knew after reading it; I wanted to be with a powerful woman.

Soon after, I began to join Ahid's circle of people who studied African and Egyptian doctrines. I learned even more about Black people's great history, which began way before the American slave trade. We became self-made scholars in that cottage. At times, we would even have definition contests, where the definition was revealed and someone would have to guess the correct word. This was the way we utilized our time, and it helped me make up for all that I had wasted.

One day I was coming from carpentry class and I saw Vern, another person who was into educating himself. I knew him from the streets as a fellow drug dealer, but he was a changed man with a positive attitude to match. It was inspirational. Vern told me about a program called Amer-I-Can, which was giving a presentation at the facility later that day. I told him I would see him at the seminar later, and went to change my clothes.

Once I got back to my cottage everybody was saying, "Mutah, the legendary football player Jim Brown's program is coming to the facility!" I had never been into sports, but I heard of him. So once I arrived at the seminar's location, which was also where the Christian services were held, there were already many people there for the presentation. I sat down and tried to imagine what to expect. Then all of a sudden, a group of Black men in suits came in and walked to the podium. We all were moved to applaud, simply because their entrance was a statement of power alone. They all sat down except for the facilitator, Shahid Watson, a serious-looking man. When he began to speak, we sat up straight and listened to the valuable wisdom he shared. I had never heard a man speak with such conviction. I imagined it was similar to being able to watch Malcolm X express priceless knowledge effortlessly. Everything around me became frozen, and I felt like Shahid was talking to me, giving me instructions on how not to get gunned down in the concrete jungle streets; the importance of making goals; and how to set obtainable and realistic ones. However, he explained that through the Amer-I-Can program, we had the chance to make a positive change. He told us that there would be a class held next week and encouraged us to join. After the seminar everyone applauded, but I felt compelled to meet him and shake his hand.

Back at the cottage, I began to imitate Mr. Watson for fun,

although it was because I liked the feeling of importance he exuded. After a while I stopped entertaining others with my role-playing, because I noticed that they were actually joking on my 'performance'. I guess it was funny, but deep inside I was serious.

It was the first time Amer-I-Can came to the facility, and I was a part of its first class. There were two classes being given at the same time, and were run by Black men who had experienced many problems and harsh realities that the inmates could relate to. Attending this program showed that I was living up to standards that I began to hold for myself. Learning and motivating myself became a natural process for me. This course exceeded my expectations, because it gave me a chance to express my fears of disparity from the only lifestyle that I had known. I had a habit of operating on the streets, which I had to acknowledge and replace with helpful qualities. Everyone in the class shared a commonality for the need of positive change. I didn't understand my deep addiction to the drug dealing until I enrolled in this course, which taught me that selling drugs was no better than using them, because I was addicted to the money. I risked and disregarded my freedom, and all the other dangers that I faced, which is what drug addicts do.

One day at the end of a session, I asked the facilitator how he would feel if someone lied or betrayed him, causing him to be arrested and incarcerated for 3 years. He pulled me to the side and asked, "Did you sell drugs?"

I said, "Yes."

He answered, "Snitching comes with the game and I don't care who tells you it doesn't. You can't pick and choose what part of the game you want to play. If you're gambling, you have to take the losses that come with the risk."

I replied, "That's real."

He continued, "By you wearing that on your shoulders, you are either going to get out and kill somebody, or they are going to kill you for trying to kill them. You will have lost twice if you go home to get revenge. Let it go before it destroys your future."

I listened to his advice, as it echoed my mother's words.

The Amer-I-Can program provided me with more hope and self-confidence. Finishing the class was just the preparation I needed for my next journey.

Not Afraid

I had served almost two years at Mountain View Correctional facility, which made me eligible to apply for the halfway house. After all I had learned in the facility, I felt ready to take this step, even though it was a risk. There were many who chose not to apply, because of fear they may violate. Many people were being returned back from the halfway house for violations they ended up committing while they were there. Most inmates had actually chosen to *stay* incarcerated, instead of taking on the responsibilities that came with living in a halfway house. Rumors had it that even a small incident could be your demise. I wasn't worried. I had become an independent thinker and wasn't interested in breaking any rules, minor or major. Besides, I enjoyed moving forward in a positive direction and it became a habit. I had to keep going. This mindset became my defense against challenges.

After I applied to live in a halfway house and was accepted, I informed my mother and a few others who were close to me. I also told those inmates who were my affiliates there after being there for almost two years. I remember clearly that a guy name Saadiq said, "Mutah, you've been reading too many books and come too far, to get sent back for any kind of petty violation." And I could honestly say I knew he was right. I had changed for the better and the life ahead of me held a whole new cast of characters.

During the process of getting into the halfway house, I was moved to another part of the facility that housed people who had minimum-level security status. I stayed there for approximately one month, and was then moved to another facility in Secaucus. This place was the melting pot for all New Jersey correctional facilities. Inmates made a pit stop there before the chance to go to a halfway house was finalized. For approximately three months, I experienced an atmosphere with men who appeared more focused about re-entering society. There were people who had been incarcerated for up to 25 years, and they were always in deep thought, appearing to silently strategize how they would function as free men, with a criminal record. The old street behaviors were not on stage in this facility, they were certainly subdued. I guess when people are truly ready for a positive transition; the idea of managing their lives becomes a priority.

While I was there, Muslims from the Nation of Islam were hyped up and excited about the major event of the Million Man March in Washington D.C. It was a phenomenon that their leader Minister Louis Farrakhan had organized a march for what everyone hoped would equal a million Black men. On the day of the event, I watched it on the television in the recreational room with a majority of Muslims. Throughout the telecast they yelled, "That's right, brother Farrakhan. They said you couldn't do it, and look at you shining!" That *Autobiography of Malcolm X* feeling hit me again. This was a historical event, and it motivated me through the promotion of honorable and positive behaviors that could exist in people. And for the journey I was traveling, The Million Man March was a great addition to my motivation.

The Affects of Incarceration

As soon as I got comfortable in the facility, it was my time to go to the halfway house. I wasn't overly anxious. I had already gone through the bulk of an emotional nightmare, and I had since learned how to manage the ranges of emotions that dwelled within myself. However, I was not *100* percent back on track and ready for the world. I still had to break habits I developed from being incarcerated. The responsibilities of paying for my shelter or other basic necessities were areas I had to take on. Incarceration slowly takes away the dependability of taking care of yourself, which is counter-productive to rehabilitation.

I've encountered men who were more comfortable with being incarcerated because their basic needs were always supplied. In addition, their normal level of functioning within greater society had been damaged, and they were totally unaware of it most of the times. In jail, there are aspects such as dialogue, slang, dress codes, and other behaviors that can become a part of one's character. Without proper maintenance, a person's social skills to function in the outside world can greatly diminish.

The inmate's self-esteem is constantly being tested, and at times broken, which keeps him in a constant battle to maintain it. The culture of incarceration can turn a man's natural instinct to be a roaming, powerful lion, into that of a temperamental pussycat. I've seen men desperately want for visits on the weekend, which is an example of how breakable their sense of self becomes. They would get a haircut, take a shower, iron their clothes and get dressed to a tee. They would painfully hope and wait for the visit, which at times would never arrive. The inmate would then get on the phone, call the person who committed this careless act of forgetfulness (in the eyes of the inmate), and say, "What happened? I can't believe you didn't come! You stood me up! Where the hell were you? Damn, I was waiting all day! Yo', I don't even feel like talking right now, because I'm mad as hell!" Try adding frustrated, sad, and lonely, too. After a few situations like this, a person's self-esteem will experience some serious damage. And that's life isn't it we all go through ups and downs? But, the inmate is not living '*life*' as we all imagine it should be. It is a different world for him or her, and to the friends and families on the 'outside' it is a world that they can always assist the inmate with some normalcy.

Then there's the case when someone tells an inmate that a clothing package or money order will be sent, and the inmate eagerly awaits his gifts. However, if the package doesn't arrive, the inmate immediately feels let down and worthless. There is, as strange as it sounds, an emotional connection to the package itself, which symbolizes a reconfirmation of love. But, when the package doesn't come, he assumes there's no more love to look forward to. "Out of sight, out of mind," is what many of these men believe their friends and families feel about them. In the end, these feelings are unhealthy and do nothing to help a man hold his head up high. It can appear to many that incarceration is free time, but it's really a major life crossroad, and possibly a catalyst for manic-depression. Correction facilities are not rehabilitation centers. This is a major misconception. However, people do have the choice to utilize their period of incarceration as a time and opportunity to change negative thinking and behaviors.

Halfway There

Finally, I arrived in Newark's Lincoln Park at the Pyramid House. I couldn't believe I was back in my hometown, and it felt good. I breathed in all that I saw around me. A new chapter in my life had begun.

"Hello, my name is Mr. Bowers and I will be your counselor while you're a resident here." Mr. Bowers, a tall, light-skinned, wavy haired and loud man, explained the rules and regulations of the halfway house. He ended the brief orientation with a blunt statement, "Don't get sent back for some dumb stuff." This halfway house advocated finding employment and enrolling in school. In a short time, I learned the house's routine and became somewhat comfortable. My mother and the rest of my family were elated that I had arrived. It was as if they had a little piece of me back at home—closer to them again.

The next time my counselor sat with me, he informed me that I had to find a job or go to school full-time. It just so happened that I applied to Essex County College when I was in the correctional facility, and had been accepted. When I told him, he said I could become a full-time student and encouraged me to get a part-time job. Before the session ended, he said, "I'm going to give you a pass for four hours, so you can go to the college." It was as if the words came out of his mouth in pure gold and in slow motion. He was letting me go out, alone. "You're going to let me out?" I stutter. But before he responded I said, "I mean, are you going to let me handle my business tomorrow?" Even that subtle incarcerated way of thinking and feeling confined had to be curved. It was more than just an opportunity to run the streets of Newark for four hours, it was a chance to begin patching my life up.

The next day I went to Essex County College and it was like heaven to feel a little freedom. I took the bus and anticipated what I would see when I arrived. There were many different people of shades and ethnicities walking through the lobby of the school. I was 20 years old and it was my very first visit to a college. The combination of freedom and seeing all of what I assumed was beautiful intelligent women, I had to go in the bathroom, wash my face, and talk to myself in the mirror. I said, "Calm down now, and find the financial aid office." My old mindset was waking up—it now had some freedom to stretch out and act foolishly. I found the financial aid office, filled out the paperwork, and the day ended as a successful one.

The other residents in the halfway house were always at work or going to school, and I really liked the positive and competitive atmosphere. If you were there for a while and couldn't find work or enroll in school, it made you appear stagnant, compared to the others living there. A few weeks later, I received a full financial aid approval. I registered for the required 12 credits and decided to take on Business Management.

I was so ready to exercise my brain. In all of my classes, I was an eager participant. I'll always remember two of my first semester classes, Health 101 and English. My Health course was at 7:00 a.m. and I learned about all of the body's phenomenal functions. I was amazed at how the body had mechanisms to heal itself, the nervous system, brain, heart, and all of the other very important organs. This process of retaining collegiate information was a wonderful challenge.

The professor of my English remedial class thought I cheated on my final exam. She explained that since I had gotten a very low grade on the initial assessment test, it was hard to believe the extremely huge difference on my final exam. In the end, she conceded that I didn't cheat, but that made me proud of my efforts to improve. Before then, my only school memories were of elementary. Forget about high school—I used that as a fashion show before I got kicked out. This college experience was a frontier I was ready to take on; my boots were laced, and my vision clear.

I continued to go to school and eventually obtained a job at a home for senior citizens, Newark's Extended Care Facility. I was an assistant recreational aide. I have always been a respectable person to elders, thanks to my mother, so it was easy for me to operate in such an environment. The low pay was compensated by the rich experience of working with some of society's wisest people, who through years of living had so much to share with others. I was exposed to the reality of how old age will transform us all, and I learned about the different ailments that can come with it too. This was the first time I had ever heard of Alzheimer's and I was able to see how it affected people. I saw beautiful pictures of some of the women and men when they were much younger, and some things I witnessed frightened me a little, because getting old looked more painful for some than others. I did enjoy working with them, because I was in the presence of wisdom. I even learned the history of the riots in Newark from one of the patients. Being employed there also gave me the opportunity to be myself, and for this I greatly appreciate that experience.

I maintained a schedule of working and going to school

for the entire time I was in the halfway house, which was approximately one year. My journey of incarceration had come to an end; my three years had been served. While I was there, only a few people came to visit me, which kept the temptations of the street life to a minimum. I had matured so much. My mother was extremely proud of me. She had witnessed the whole ordeal, and we had survived through it together.

Determined, but Unemployed

Upon leaving the halfway house, I had a major addition to my life. My daughter Indira Wisdom was born just days before my exit. I was a father again (The pregnancy occurred during a home pass). I then had to decide whether I should continue going to school with a part-time job, or get full-time employment. I chose to leave Essex County College and get a full-time job. The reality was that, at the age of 21, I had two children. Leaving school took a chip out of my spirit because I had felt hopeful and upwardly mobility in my productive activities. But my daughter took priority over my personal feelings; I did what I felt was responsible at the time.

It was 1997 and I had to find a job as soon as possible, because my past drug dealing skills were becoming more and more attractive. I couldn't find a job anywhere, or at least not fast enough. The many educational pursuits I was involved in throughout my incarceration suppressed the materialism factor that was within me, but now I was on my own. I began to utilize some of my skills to manage those old behaviors, so that I wouldn't give in to the memories of my former lifestyle. I occupied myself by reading books and writing down thoughts of some of the things I had learned during the last three years. My favorite book, "*Things Fall Apart*," was one of the books I read during that painful free time. I also wrote often about race issues, relationships, and poetry.

At that time, I was still developing my thoughts and learning how to function in the greater society. Here is an excerpt from one of my writings at the time:

All the men and women of the world must first put the truth about themselves on the table to the other person in the relationship, whether the relationships are with your mother, father, sister, brother, wife, or girlfriend. If the other person accepts you after the truth has been revealed, it is up to them to continue in the relationship. The power behind this action is that the other person will love you for you. The response of your realness will be like a magnetic force. In order for this powerful act to take place, you have to know yourself.

I wrote many things similar to this in order to keep myself stimulated. I wrote as if I had an audience. Sometimes when I read my old notes, it's funny because I can hear that militant tone, which reflected my alertness and desire to move forward. I was doing whatever I could to manage the corruption lurking inside.

When I was in the halfway house, I exchanged telephone numbers with a guy who worked for a long distance company in the telemarketing division. He often came back to the facility bragging about how his talkative nature made him money. The boasting, especially about the money, had stayed in my mind ever since, so I called his house. He told me the company was hiring in many different departments and shared what the duties of the vacancies were. He suggested I call them quickly to get an interview.

The first person I called happened to be an associate I knew who was recently released from incarceration. I thought maybe he want to get a 9 to 5. When I called the company the next day, they connected me to the quality assurance department, who was holding interviews that week. The interviews were set. My acquaintance drove us to Bloomfield where the company was located. Upon our arrival, we spoke briefly to the hiring manager, who also asked us to do a trial run that day, to see if we wanted the position. Our duties were to listen to the recorded tapes of the telemarketers and confirm that the sales were made legally. We agreed to stay and test the waters. At first it appeared simple, but after listening to cassette tapes for two hours straight, it was pretty draining. After our trial day, which included finding errors on the tapes, we were hired on the spot.

As we drove home on the Garden State Parkway, my associate said, “I can’t do it. I can’t listen to tapes for eight hours. What about you?”

I looked at him and said, “I’m going to give it a try.” I wanted to be in the driver’s seat and be the engineer of my life—peer-pressure and my old ways would have to take a back seat.

Entrepreneurship Calls

For about two years, I caught the bus to work everyday. After one year of working in the quality assurance department, I was transferred over to the warehouse department in West Orange. The skills I learned from the quality assurance department were of little use to me at the time. As I listened to tapes all day, I only could think of ways to make money. I began doodling and drawing my ideas out on paper while I appeared to be working. I wasn't the best artist but I learned some basic drawing techniques from my oldest brother when I was 10-years-old.

One day I had a vision. I sketched an ethnic-looking woman blowing wind out of her mouth, which rotated a globe that she had in the palm of her hand. Now I just needed someone to put an artist's final touch on it. Surprisingly, there was a co-worker in the same office that drew cartoons. I gave him the sketch and he brought it to life. That day, I wrote my first contract, which required him to relinquish any and all ownership of the image, and paid him $100. I had the art printed on some T-shirts and started my first business. The shirts did sell, but my customer base was limited since I didn't have enough money to largely invest in my products. I eventually put the business on pause, but continued to think about more ways to make money. I knew I liked making money, so I tried my best to channel the energy in a positive direction, in order to stay motivated—legally.

My next business idea soon followed. At the time, Newark's craze was that people were buying "Brick City" T-shirts. A guy named Ron Muhammad supplied the demand of these T-shirts. He was doing exactly what I wanted to do, except in abundance. Ron and I eventually became close business associates. I couldn't do Brick City T-shirts because it wasn't my original idea, but I began sketching the letters "BC" until I came up with something that I felt was creative and worthy enough to be considered a business endeavor. By then I had become acquainted with artists who could make my sketches come to life. A Puerto-Rican guy named Elvis perfected my design, and I named it Brick Collection. I immediately had T-shirts printed and people loved them. Brick Collection was now my own line of urban wear. I soon began to sell hats, sweat-hoods, and sweatshirts, which the public also received well.

During that year, some people I knew were having a show with R&B group Jagged Edge and hip-hop artist AZ, at the Robert Treat Hotel in Newark. My clothing line was pretty popular on a local level, so they asked me to feature it at the show. This was my big break, so I invested in endless color schemes on T-shirts, embroidery on v-neck sweaters, and many other things.

On the night of the show, I packed all of my products into the trunk and 'a business associate' drove us down to the venue. We almost would have made it, but less than a mile from our destination on Washington Street, we crashed into another car after mistakenly running a red light. I was knocked unconscious, due to my face hitting the dashboard and the strong impact.

I had prepared such an array of products for the show's attendees and I never even made it that night. This was the main event that I hoped would have produced a positive turn for my business. I was so upset that I didn't make it, and of course my highly motivated spirit was broken. The accident damaged my back and nerves temporarily. I even had to get physical therapy for months. I was very fortunate to have survived.

There is a theory by the name of Learned Helplessness. The process of learned helplessness can happen over a period of what some may view as constant deprivation. For instance: There was a lab test conducted with dogs. The dogs were shocked and then ran out the gate. The shocking continued but the gate would not open. Learned helplessness came when the dog got shocked and the gate stayed opened but the animal did not move. The dog had to be dragged out of the cage. The feelings of learned helplessness seemed to be creeping on me after that night of let down and lost dreams. This learned helpless is easy to obtain for those that have experience having a lack of things throughout their lives. I shook it off and continued to think and plan for a new direction.

I did what any accident victim would do; I sued the driver of the car. After I finished going to the chiropractor for almost a year, I settled out of court for $13,000, which came right on time. In fact, I had just gotten laid off from my job with the telemarketing company and was collecting unemployment. I wasn't selling any T-shirts, because I did not have any investment money.

Since I knew I had some money coming in from the lawsuit, I began looking for a vacant storefront that I could rent. I also began scouting for a business partner. My desires to get more money directed me toward someone I knew from the past, who was currently selling drugs. I considered him as a business partner, because I knew he would have money to invest without a problem. He respected me, because of my street credibility, and also, due to my recent popular clothing company. Q-Bee was originally from Hawthorne Avenue but by the time I came home from being incarcerated, he was dealing on Renner Avenue. We talked about a store that was available on Chancellor Avenue.

A Very Bad Decision

We agreed to invest $7,000 each in a clothing store. I was going to take care of the business side, while he continued hustling. We rented the store, which was on the corner of Chancellor Avenue and Leslie Street. I thought it was a good location because Weequahic High School was just down the street. The store needed some repairs, which slowed down the grand opening, but finally by the summer of '99, I could say I had my own business. However, my disparities and hopes led me to make that irrational decision of having a drug dealer as a business partner. A decision that later proved to have been a very bad decision.

The idea of being my own boss was uplifting, especially after the car accident deflated my world. During the time I was waiting for the store to get fixed, I was a single man, and I had two children who lived with their mother in Newark. I was in my 20's and had become stylish and flashy again. I was an entrepreneur and my business partner had a Porsche that I sported at times. I was on the party scene often and women were quite interested. I had my own apartment and although I was a father, I lived a bachelor's life. I did still have high standards regarding meeting the intelligent woman of my dreams.

One day as I was going through my files, I found the telephone number of a beautiful young lady I had met months ago. Her name was Ayesha, and I met her at an Avon Avenue bar called Professionals. I remember the first time I saw her. I had just walked in and there she was, across the room. I walked past once and got some eye contact—and then I said, "You are so brown."

She replied, "You are, too."

I sensed a little sarcasm there, so I moved further into her space to ask her name and if she lived in the area. She told me that her friends had convinced her to check out the bar—although she expressed it wasn't a normal practice. And it was obvious because she was just chillin', drinking cranberry-pineapple juice, as if she were on a resort and not in the middle of the 'hood. It turned out that she was on a break from Morgan State University where she was a student. I was attracted to her style, so I began to say things that made her feel comfortable with my presence.

The conversation went on for a while, and I eventually gave her my business card and telephone number. She gave me the privilege of having dinner with her once, just before she went back to college in Baltimore, Maryland. Because she was busy with college out-of-state, and I was working on a business, we didn't properly maintain a long distance relationship.

So an entire year went passed and I called her to see if she was available. She had just graduated from college. We talked on the phone extensively and decided to go to New York City to eat. We went to an Argentinean and Brazilian restaurant in SoHo. Amid the serene atmosphere, we got very deep into conversations spanning so many areas. Before we left, I knew I wanted to have a serious relationship with her. She then took me to a place called Nuyorican Café. This was the first time I had ever seen live poetry. There was a band, different poets, and even an actor, Mums from the HBO series "Oz", who performed. I'll never forget that night because it was truly the start of a new beginning.

My store, Brick Collection, was finally renovated. I went to

New York to buy the clothes from the wholesale district, and equipped the store with a sound system. Ayesha had even helped me stock the shelves. By then I had fallen in love with her. Ironically, she was placed to work just down the street in the high school, when she applied to the Newark Board of Education for a teaching position. I was so proud of my accomplishment, even though part of it involved Q-B, who was still selling drugs. I brought my mother and children to see the store, and they rejoiced in my happiness as well. Of course, no one, not even Ayesha, knew that part of my business had been funded with drug money.

Back on the Block

The store was ready to open, but my business partner began to get involved with the operations. He proposed that we buy out the thrift shop next-door and not open our business until we combined the two stores. He pleaded until he convinced me this step would make us much more money. Once again, greed had got in the way of good decision making. I yielded to the situation. My partner offered the thrift shop's owner $2,000 to move out, which he accepted.

At this point, I believed he was serious about taking the business to a higher level, so I was all for it. However, the price of combining these stores would cost us tens of thousands of dollars. Q-B told me that he would have to make the money on the streets in order to pay for the construction. He eventually began to suggest that if I came out to hustle with him, we'd have the store opened quicker. The thought of having more money snuffed out the coping and leadership abilities that I had acquired. Eventually, I started selling drugs with him on Renner Avenue. After all I had learned the hard way; I was once again, my worst enemy.

After a few weeks, I confessed this to Ayesha. Upset and disgusted, tearfully she expressed that I was worth more than being a drug dealer and that I was one of the few men whom she respected. The image I had presented to her was one of a young, strong-minded, positive entrepreneur that ascended the struggle of the streets. She continued to present factual consequences to my actions such as risking my freedom and fatherhood, and other issues that I obviously disregarded for my own selfish wants. Her last words to me were, "I can't be with you."

Those words were motivating for two reasons; I didn't want to lose my girl and I never had a girl that didn't just go with the flow. I asked her to come back to the store with me so we could continue to talk about our future, which I knew would be ruined if I didn't give up the streets for good. When we arrived at the store, she noticed most of the clothes were gone. I told her that while my partner and I made money hustling, we begun wearing the goods. She again began to explain how my master plan for a bigger clothing store blinded me to the obvious. She insisted that I was moving backwards. There was no money going back into the store. I was wearing the products that were purchased to make a profit, and I was still shelling out rent money for a store that I didn't own. Nothing was adding up. Every one of her words was breaking down my old mindset. Suddenly, I was more aware of my place in the struggle to regain my sanity.

That next week, my business partner was fatally shot in the head. This was a tragic situation because he had a newborn son. However, the streets of Newark were and are still filled with young Black men that seem to hate each other for many different reasons. In many neighborhoods, the "street dramas" were marked with thrills and chills that involved murder. Not the television kind, where the victim is miraculously revived, but the kind that leaves families and love ones to mourn forever. I had to leave the streets before I was next in line for a Perry's Funeral home finale.

The manner, in which these young Black men get murdered, is the filthiest way to die. Some cultures are known to go to the scene where one of their kind has been killed, even if accidentally, and they scrape the blood off the ground.

They believe their blood is too precious to be wasted and dishonored. My generation appears to have a lack of concern, to say the least, for the well being of one another. The atmosphere of hatred and rage leads to bloodshed. This tragedy of Q-B's death hit too close to home.

After, and even before my partner's death, business at the store was slow. The poor, surrounding community couldn't be counted on as loyal customers. Profits were low, and it became a discouraging struggle. Nevertheless, I tried to add all kinds of attractions: video games, five-dollar photo-shots, and even bootleg CD's. My efforts were so noticeable that my Jewish landlord lent me $500—I was accepting a loan from the person I was paying rent to. Eventually, I was forced to close the store. I felt as though I lost, again. The biggest mistake was opening a business with a drug dealer and believing that it would lead to a prosperous venture. There were too many risks.

By 1999, I had decided to refocus and refine my life with no flashy cars, no hustler associates, and unfortunately no plans. It was just me—from the bottom up. Ayesha and I now lived together, which was a breathing space for me. It was a place I could speak about my dreams, share my strong opinions, and share strength with her. She even became my employment counselor, asking me questions about the types of jobs I might like or could tolerate. I didn't have a clue because I desperately wanted to own my own business. Ayesha explained to me that owning a business was not a realistic idea at the time, because I didn't have the money. Still slightly blinded by ignorance, I told her that I might know where I could get some money, because there were people who owed me from the drug game. She looked at me as if I were speaking Greek and shook her head. Then very assertively, she asked me not to make the streets an option anymore. She wanted me to put all the energy I had into developing a legal and productive future. Truthfully, I was scared because once again, I was starting over.

The positive lifestyle and hope Ayesha and I tried to foster helped both of us overcome challenges and reach new heights. We were never satisfied with just enough. These characteristics helped me in my journey to find a job. I didn't know what kind of work I wanted to do, so I just approached different companies. I applied to the Marriott hotel at the Newark airport through their phone-automated system, which resulted in an interview. Ayesha prepped me by asking me interview questions and suggesting what I should wear. She also helped me create my first resume, and even highlighted my experience as a former retail storeowner. She translated those qualities into attributes an employer would be attracted to.

I went on the interview and the hiring manager told me that my respect, confidence, warm spirit and proactive abilities impressed him. I ended up getting the job at the hotel's kitchen. It didn't last long. I then move on to a rental car service in the Newark Liberty Airport as a transporter of cars from Newark airport to New York City. But, I didn't like the idea of speeding up and down the highway. I felt that I was worth more than risking my life on the highway everyday. My next gig was as a bread deliveryman in Edison, N.J. That job was really interesting. My workday started at 3:30 AM in order to be in Edison at 4:00 AM. My duty was to pick the orders for the supermarkets and local stores, and then stack the bread in these long humongous trucks. If I didn't stack them properly, the tall bread mountains, which were on dollies, would roll around while I was driving. When I finally arrived at these stores, I had to count all the stacks with the managers, which was just backbreaking. Needless to say, I didn't stick with that job for too long.

One day I was looking through the newspaper and saw an ad for a salesman. I thought maybe I had a knack to be a successful salesman, so I called. The vague ad turned out to be for an opportunity based in Pennsylvania. It was a company that sold home windows plus installation and offered a compensation package with paid training. I took on the challenge and accepted their offer of employment. I drove back and forth for many miles every day for two weeks, only to go into strange neighborhoods in an attempt to convince people that our windows were the best in the industry. I lugged around a presentation binder, samples of glass, and an electronic measuring tape. You can imagine my disgust when my first paycheck was a mere $175. I did not know they would deduct the cost of my sales materials, nor did they highlight this information. I certainly felt like a jerk. Of course, I quit right after that paycheck of peanuts.

As I searched for yet another job, my father died of cancer. The experience was very difficult; mainly because I knew my mother would be left without a partner and a husband from whom she endured a lot of strife. After 27 years, he was leaving her alone in the world, and I was angry and saddened on her behalf. I was my mother's rock throughout the whole ordeal. I became the spokesperson and greeter for the family during the wake and the funeral. After the funeral, I had a long discussion with my mother. I suggested that she leave New Jersey and go down south, where her other siblings lived. I paid for her Greyhound ticket and she was on her way to Phoenix City, Alabama. It was a painful life-changing event for me. I didn't want to see her go, but I knew she would be happier if she went. Luckily, Ayesha was there to give me the support I needed, which helped me accept all that was taking place.

Choosing a Career

Not too much longer after this, Ayesha told me that she dreamt I was talking in front of a group of men and when I finished speaking, they all came one by one to hug me. She said that since I usually liked to give long, but well-intentioned speeches and I cared about people, that maybe I should be a counselor. It didn't sound like a bad idea and it was worth investigating. We eventually found a position at a drug treatment facility in Lincoln Park in Newark, which was right next to the halfway house I once lived in. I secured an interview and was offered a position as a counselor's aide, but the salary was too low, so I turned down the job. I wasn't being picky, like I had jobs lined up. I just wanted to be compensated fairly for my efforts, as my last job experience taught me a real good lesson.

Still looking for a job, I ran into an old friend, Keith Hooper, who told me that his job was hiring counselors. He explained to me that the facility where he was a supervisor was a part of the community correction industry. It housed men who were coming home from incarceration and making a transition into New Jersey halfway houses. The job paid well, but the hardest part would probably be that I might know some of the residents there. It was important that I had clear boundaries if I wanted to explore the opportunity.

The facility, Talbot Hall Assessment Center, was in Kearny, and Hooper ensured me an interview with Mr. Spruill the Chief of Operations. During the interview, Mr. Spruill, explained that I would be working in the capacity of security, although there would be no bars. I would have to wear a shirt and tie everyday, which I didn't mind. He explained that I could make a career out of this field, if I went back to school and became a state Certified Alcohol and Drug Counselor (CADC). At the time I didn't know what this was, and besides, I was more interested in simply getting the job. Mr. Spruill said I would be welcomed aboard as soon as they ran a criminal background check on me. I went home feeling like a winner. I couldn't wait to tell Ayesha the good news. And just as I thought, she was elated that the dream she had was aligned with all that was taking place.

A week later, someone from the company called and asked that I come in and fill out some additional paperwork. When I arrived, I was sent to the facility's library. As I waited, an officer from the Essex County Sheriff's Department walked in and asked, "Are you A. Williams?"

I replied, "No, but I have used that name as an alias in the past."

The officer then said, "Do you have any warrants?"

"No sir," I answered.

"We are going to have to fingerprint you," he said assertively.

The officer fingerprinted me and learned that the warrant wasn't for my arrest. I stayed in the room until another officer brought in the mug shot of the suspect they wanted. When the authorities saw that it wasn't my face, they apologized for the mix up, but noted that they had to be sure I wasn't their guy. After the annoying ordeal, I was hired as an operations counselor. That was a big scare. I went home and told Ayesha about everything I went through that day, and she was relieved that everything worked in my favor. I was moving further away from learned helplessness.

Talbot Hall was a place that educated its residents about the affects of drugs, alcohol, and criminal behaviors, before they were assigned to a halfway house. My job was to secure the building and monitor the residents' behaviors. I had to focus on interacting with them in a positive way, because ultimately I was a part of their treatment process. I had to enforce many rules upon the residents. No cursing. No fighting. Keep your shirt tucked in your pants. No hats. Don't display threatening behaviors. These rules supposedly would assist them in their transition back into society. I knew, however, that it would take much more than a tucked-in shirt to get ahead.

I started seeing some residents I knew and the majority of the time they said, "Mutah, I'm proud to see that you changed your life and started working." This was gratifying to hear, and I became even more interested in the facility's objectives regarding trying to change some of the negative behaviors of the residents. The facility's mission caught my interest because I knew personally that change wasn't easy.

One day when I was working in the cafeteria, a resident said to me, "I can't change from being negative."

I replied, "If you say you can't, you won't. Try saying, 'I can do it'."

Before he could respond, a co-worker said to me, "What's up Tyrone? I heard what you said to that resident and I'm going to put in a good word for you, so that you can become a unit counselor upstairs where you can be even more of an asset to the residents. That was some quick therapy that you gave that resident."

This meant he wanted to recommend me for a promotion. In the units, residents had primary counselors who helped them directly with their recovery process. The units were like their home base in the facility, so it's where they were most comfortable. The Unit Counselors also interacted with the residents on a more personal level, in addition to taking count of them at different times of the day. Writing and documenting residents' behaviors was also very important, and I'd be doing that as well.

Gotta Give Back

While working on the unit, I learned more about primary counselors' responsibilities. I observed them giving seminars on behavioral change and drug recovery techniques. They held smaller groups with the residents in order to encourage them to disclose past behaviors and the lessons they'd learned from bad decision-making. I inquired more about what a CADC was and found out that the lengthy process of the certification would give a person the vital information needed to function effectively as a primary counselor in any drug treatment facility. The certification required many educational/classroom hours; 6,000 practical hours of internship in a treatment facility (which was three years of full-time work); a three-hour written examination; a case study; and an oral examination in which you were questioned rigorously. I decided to make this field a career, so I went back to Essex County College to fulfill the educational requirements of the certification. My employment hours at Talbot Hall could be utilized as the practical hours, which made me excited to embark on a career, finally.

I worked at Talbot Hall for two years before I resigned. Within two years my life had changed drastically. As a Unit Counselor on the Tranquility Unit, I learned a lot from many other professionals. I learned to facilitate educational seminars and lectures on topics such as anger and stress management, drug relapse and coping skills, criminal behavior and cognitive/behavioral methods. The work ethics I gained were among the most valuable assets I attained at the time.

A major goal I accomplished before leaving was that I

fulfilled all of the educational requirements for the certification and also passed the written examination, which was given at Montclair University. My full energy and focus were on developing a career, I knew I had to man-up. My enrollment and participation in college escalated my abilities to perform my duties as a Unit Counselor while preparing me to be a primary counselor, which was another step up. I took extensive classes in psychology, sociology and criminal justice, studying hard at night, and passing with flying colors. My affinity for education was awakened and I developed new techniques to study, which is why I excelled.

Ayesha thought I was being too hard on myself, but it worked for me. I would thoroughly read all of the information I had to study once, before writing it all down word for word. The process involved a combination of senses to retain and understand my subject matter. I had many late night cups of coffee, but it was all for the best. For instance, the three-hour written examination for the certification was so difficult that 80% of people who took it for the first time failed. I met people who had flunked seven times, and even heard other stories of how professionals who had PhDs chose to stop taking the test after they just couldn't pass. The first time I took the examination, I passed. My co-workers were pretty surprised because I wasn't a veteran in the field of Substance Abuse Treatment. For me, it was proof that my hard work was paying off. And speaking of pay—I had resigned because another facility offered me a better position with a higher salary. It was a business decision because after all, I did have two children to support.

The staff gave me a luncheon at Olive Garden on my last day. They reminisced on how supportive I was as a member of the team. They would especially remember me for my no-nonsense phrase "Keep it effective!" It was a successful experience, and I was walking the walk of an effective, responsible man: a hero unto myself.

Jumping the Broom

The biggest accomplishment and change in those two years had nothing to do with my professional life. Eventually, Ayesha and I got married. It was a surprise to many because we were a young couple. She was 24 and I was 27 at the time. The truth is that we came from totally opposite backgrounds and some people may have been skeptical. She graduated from Science High School in Newark, and I sold drugs throughout my high school years. She graduated from Morgan State University, and I was incarcerated for 36 months. She graduated with a degree in English/Journalism and I graduated from the School of Hard Knocks with a degree in Streetology. She was raised as a Muslim and I never attended a Masjid in my life before I met her. There were many opposites, but we both shared intense ambition and determination. Other areas where we connected were: that as members of the hip-hop generation, we enjoyed artists like Nas and Queen Latifah; we cracked up having conversations about De La Soul, the Daisy Age, and the Golden Age of Puff Daddy. We both liked to analyze world issues and shared the same views about raising a strong family.

We got married at The Hackensack Meadowlands Environmental Center in Lyndhurst. Many people came to our wedding, including my mother who flew up from down south. She was so proud of her baby boy. Ayesha's friends came from Baltimore, Maryland, and Washington, D.C. to support us in preparing for the big day. Her parents owned an ice cream parlor in East Orange for many years and were well known in the Muslim community. The fact that their daughter was getting married was a big deal. The venue we chose for our ceremony was perfect. There was an auditorium where we exchanged vows and a reception hall that was on the water at the other end of the property, which her mother and friends beautifully decorated. The wedding turned out to be a big social festivity. Ayesha even had the wedding announced in the Star-Ledger newspaper. It was one a pleasure.

I was then hired by a facility named The Kintock Day Reporting Center that was in Newark, as a Drug and Alcohol Counselor. I dealt with a male and female population who reported to the center daily, as require by their parole officers. At the Day Reporting Center, I maintained a caseload of 14-16 clients, developed treatment plans for the parole-mandated clients, and utilized assessment instruments. I conducted referrals and maintained community resources. I also held seminars on drugs and alcohol, relapse prevention, peer pressure, stress management, S.M.A.R.T. Recovery (Self Management and Recovery Training) sessions, and group therapy. My career developed greatly and my professionalism was polished.

I was in the final requirement phase for the CADC certification. I had to submit a case study and sit through the oral examination. When I arrived to take it, I saw that the people who would be questioning me all had badges that read PhD. It was intimidating to say the least. My study techniques, however, had helped to retain my case study in the areas of screening, intake, orientation, treatment planning, individual counseling, group counseling, family counseling, case management, crisis intervention, client education, referral, consultation, and reports/record keeping. The exam was recorded with a timer in my face.

It was one of the most grueling and intense experiences in my educational journey. I never had to retain so much information and then articulate it back accurately and comfortably. There was no 'fake it 'til you make it' for this certification. Finally, after three years of practicum hours and all the late night studying, I was a New Jersey Certified Alcohol and Drug Counselor. I felt validated as a professional, and certainly as an expert in my field.

Stigmas and Setbacks

In the field of social services, I think everyone should have outside interests or hobbies because you can easily experience a stressful burnout. I began to feel the weight of the client's constant issues. Although I liked my career, I am human, and at times, the pressure was a lot to handle. My family life was good and we helped each other with spiritual wellness, but I wanted something especially for me, because I felt a void. I began to search my mental rolodex for answers. I knew I had an entrepreneurial element and still had a need to be active in the business world. I decided to pursue my New Jersey Real Estate License. I enrolled in a Weichert Real Estate school in Clifton, NJ where I took classes on Saturdays and Sundays for approximately nine weeks. The course was stimulating and I had something to look forward to every weekend, which was gratifying. I was active in class and had no problem applying my studying skills to learn the contents of the thick real estate course book, filled with laws and technical information. I was extremely focused and in the end, I successfully completed the course and was prepared to take the state real estate examination.

I took the test at a location in Millburn. The test covered countless regulations that were rarely used in the field. Before I took the test, there was a question about whether I had any criminal convictions. I paused for a second before answering and hoped that my past wouldn't spoil my chances of becoming a real estate salesman. I answer the question "yes" for criminal convictions and proceeded to take the test. Another winning step—I passed the exam. I did find out soon after, that I would have to contact the Real

Estate Commission in Trenton because of my criminal background. It wasn't what I wanted to hear, but I had to move forward if this was what I wanted.

I contacted the Real Estate Commission, and was informed that I had to gather all documents in relation to my convictions and send them to the Commission, along with a letter explaining the convictions. They also wanted six letters of recommendation. I obtained all of my Judgments of Convictions, which are county-issued documents that states a person's crimes, convictions and whether any jail time was served. I gathered letters from close associates that I had the pleasure of meeting over the years such as school principals, college professors, and some highly credible co-workers. I mailed all that they required and waited for a response.

Reality was closing in on me. I began to get discouraged because I felt as if I just couldn't escape my past criminal history. Here it was almost a decade later from the day I was convicted, and I still had to prove myself to society. Finally, I received a response and it was requested that I come down to Trenton, NJ in order to face the Real Estate Commissioners for a hearing. I became so stressed-out that I took off a few days from work. I didn't like the feeling of having a limited life. The idea of people making decisions on whether or not I was worthy enough to get a piece of the American dream was a total turn-off. My thoughts were scattered, and I was itching with anxiety. However, I knew I had to focus and make plans. Until I knew what I was up against, I had to continue forward. I began my strategy by writing a long statement about why I should have the opportunity to possess a real estate license. I also asked Ayesha to come with me as a character witness.

On the day of the hearing, Ayesha and I took the train down to Trenton. When we arrived, we witnessed another individual make a plea to obtain his license, and once they drilled him with questions, he was granted a probationary license. I was then called in to sit in front of the panel of. I was nervous, but I ensured that my body language didn't show it. I sat in front of the Commissioners and read my statement, which helped me express myself clearly under such pressure.

The panel basically wanted to know, "Why should we allow you on the boat?" I informed them that my wife, who was my character witness, would give them even more reason to consider me as a candidate. One of the commissioners jokingly stated that my wife would naturally say only good things about me, but he welcomed her comments, which was a good thing. Ayesha spoke a little about, her background and explained that she didn't know me when I was out in the streets or incarcerated, which was true. To her, my criminal background almost seemed unreal, she insisted. She passionately gave the panel insight on whom I was in the present, which really what mattered most.

My wife and I were performing like we were hosting a talk show, and the commissioners were quite entertained with us. When the questioning was over, they asked us to step out of the room in order to discuss my case. It was like the longest wait in my life, maybe because they had my future in their hands, if only for that day. They finally asked me to return to the room and informed me that I would receive my real estate license on the condition I paid off an old parole fine of $2,300. I had no idea I even had a fine—I had never received the bill or notice. But I didn't let that take my joy. It was the gateway to another credential that I worked hard for and deserved. I just wanted to live without all the stress and strife that seemed to be directed at me. While I was relieved to have a shot at getting the license, I wondered, "Will the uphill battle bring me to a grand level one day?" I feared the frustration within me would explode like a ticking time bomb. The person I had grown to be, however, strongly believed that this was a challenge I would surely overcome.

And Baby Makes Three

It was a special morning when Ayesha called me to the bathroom and asked to read a pregnancy test. It was positive. We shared a tearful hug and began talking about how we first met and how dreamlike it was that we were now going to share a baby. She told me how confident she felt with me being the leader of the family. Though she was a bit concerned, because I had two other children and she didn't know how things were going to be in a blended family. My baby's mother was giving a little drama at the time.

There were many things we had to prepare for in this new reality. We immediately made plans for Ayesha to take a year off from work once the baby was born. I bought her a juicing machine and for the entire first trimester of her pregnancy, I made her fresh juice every morning. It was a beautiful time.

During the pregnancy, we found out that we were having a little girl, and my wife was on cloud nine. Armed with an excellent doctor, we took Lamaze classes at Saint Barnabas Hospital in Livingston, where she planned to give birth. The class gave me a good idea of what would happen in the delivery room. This was the first pregnancy I was fully involved in, because I was unfortunately incarcerated when my other two children were born. It was a blessing.

One May 31, 2005, we were hanging curtains in our East Orange apartment, when my wife said, "My water broke."

I asked, "How do you know?"

She just looked at me, and I put two and two together (she could feel it). We called her friends and her parents with the news.

The time had come and I promised myself that I wouldn't lose control due to my excitement. Her hospital bag was already packed at the door: a six-pack of Gatorade, clothes, books to read, and important papers including our birth plan were ready to go. We also took a portable boom box with a mixed CD she especially prepared for the delivery. Once we arrived at the hospital, we were directed to the ward where the stars were born. My wife breathed through her contractions, which were intensifying. Once we were settled and the music softly played in the delivery room, the excitement in the air was clear. The nurse informed us that the baby would possibly arrive the following morning.

It was June 1st, and Ayesha's doctor arrived, prepared for the big moment. It was time to get down to business—we had a baby coming. The opportunity to witness my child being born was a natural high like no other. My daughter Imaara Malkia was born to Pharoah Sanders' song "The Creator Has a Master Plan".

I chose to get a second job at the Field House in East Orange as a part-time case aide, so that Ayesha could take a year off from work. Life had evolved into what I defined as a beautiful struggle. I had become a polished professional who worked with the criminal justice population, of which I was once a part. I also felt that my work experience gave me the ability to demand more money. I would set interviews with other companies and go during my lunch break, just to find out what they were offering as a salary. Now that I was a state Certified Alcohol and Drug Counselor, I was in a position where it was inevitable that I could obtain a higher salary. I had to put my business hat on and market my capabilities.

After a few weeks of interviews, I was hired at Delaney Hall Treatment Center in Newark. The salary fit was good, so I put in a two-week resignation with my current job. By the time I left that job, I had made some positive developments. My proactive abilities and support I gave to the staff, earned me an Employee of the Month honor, for which I received a plaque and a monetary bonus. By then I had also painfully paid off the $2,300 parole fine from 10 years ago, and received my real estate license.

On my last day, my co-workers gave me a surprise party, and they talked about all the times that I made them laugh without even trying. They were good people. As the day ended, I sat in my office thinking about how I was transitioning into these jobs as if I had been doing it all my life. I began to think about the positive lifestyle that I was blessed to live and how I knew so many people who were still struggling with trying to change their negative behaviors. I chose this field as a career because at-risk young men and women need to see someone like them developing a positive life. Most importantly, they need to know they have the chance to move beyond unsatisfactory past lifestyle, into something more fulfilling.

I started my new job at Delaney Hall Treatment Center, which was also a population of men who were confined but were receiving treatment for drugs, alcohol and criminal behaviors. By this time I had had four years of experience, so I was ready to roll. This experience was similar, yet different from my previous positions, which was the reason I accepted the position. The more professional experiences you obtain the more effective the resume will appear. I enjoyed all of my many new duties, as well as, the higher salary. For the three years I worked there at Delaney Hall, and the most important skill I learned was how to work effectively manage and operate under pressure.

V for Victory

One day in the mail, I received a letter from the State of New Jersey Division of Consumer Affairs, in care of the Alcohol and Drug Counselor Committee. I was informed that since I had a criminal history, I would have to submit more information about my background in order to maintain my CADC credentials. The initial Professional Board that I received my certification from was taken over by the NJ Consumer of Affairs/State Attorney Generals Office.

When I read the letter I expressed frustration, "I can never put my past mistakes behind me because it continues to be an issue, no matter how professional I become." Then I smiled at the opportunity to prove that I was a law-abiding citizen, in order to move on with my life. My progression was worth such a small effort. A date was scheduled for me to appear in front of the committee to explain my criminal history. The aggravation within almost caused me to pout, kick, and scream about how unfair it was that people kept questioning my integrity. I chose to manage my resentment so I could once again beat the odds and proclaim myself a winner.

This hearing was located downtown Newark and I was ready for the war. However, when I entered the room with the committee, my confidence dropped a notch. I was hit with reality. They were all there for a mental battle, and I was the underdog. The atmosphere became even more intimidating once the Deputy Attorney General introduced herself. It was like a scene from a movie. I prepared thoroughly before I came, because my livelihood was at stake. I had more to lose here, as this was my primary source of income, unlike my real estate license.

The Deputy Attorney General began to speak about the purpose of the hearing, and the court reporter started typing. I quickly glanced at him and said in a quiet voice, "Damn, this is serious." The deputy's first words were, "Explain to me about the year of 1993 because it seems that was a rough year for you." That was the perfect time for me to pull out my material I had prepared to read. At that time, I highlighted some of my past inner struggles that I've begun to overcome. I gave a description of how my life at once was controlled by materialism, and linked it to my growth process and keen ability to be the ultimate manager of my life. I had evidence of my professional background, honors, certificates, my education, and the fact that I had won a similar challenge with the New Jersey Real Estate Commission. My confident attitude showed them that I was the wrong person to dethrone.

The day of that hearing was indeed a successful one. I eventually received my new certification and I'm pleased with all that it represents. I'm on the boat; in fact, I'm steering it, whether through choppy waters, calm waves, or unpredictable tides. I will never again be hindered by my unhealthy desires; I will continue to sail forth toward new horizons. And thus, I believe is how we should all approach life – The beautiful struggle.

Part Two

Homeless and Separated

In the book, "48 Laws of Power," it warns to not let your victory be your demise. The celebration that accompanies success has the ability to blind a man from the inevitable challenges that are closer to his reality than he can respond to with swiftness. Glory has to be an event that takes place in the midst of planning for the next great idea to be produced. Jay-z has a song titled, "On to the next one," which expressed to me that there is no time to waste in an unconscious state of prolonged feelings of victory.

I was a victim to my worst enemy, which translates to the inner-me. After a few victories, I began to feel and think I was that winner and it was all unfolding. Yes I was working my butt off and obtained results, but God wasn't done. I lost conscious for a minute that there were more glories and stories of struggles waiting for my best-self to arrive. Boy did I need a mentor at the time.

That's when the partying started and I mean wild ones. I was the poster child for 'King Baby', because I felt entitled to do whatever I wanted to do and things began to fall apart. I began to come in the house later and later, until a point of no show. This non-caring behavior mixed with the negative self-talk that I kept playing in my head, were the ingredients for destruction. The thoughts were, "Nobody understands the challenges I've faced," "I had to make it out of the streets and take on a marriage, man all this was too much," "I deserve more and it keeps getting harder for me." Believe me family, my thinking was not totally irrational, I just had no one to talk to and the negative self-talk just became too loud in my head. It is said that most distracting noise, is the noise inside your head.

Ayesha shouted, "You are being disrespectful to this house! You are coming in late and doing whatever you want to do these days! You are not yourself anymore! And who is this Jewish woman that you invited to a convention?" I started to say something before I got cut off, "I'm just trying to network because..." She screamed, "Get out!" That was the first time I'd ever heard that from her and I couldn't believe what I was experiencing. I looked at her, sat down and began to cry like a child who had done something really bad. She sat next to me and also began to cry but stood firm about me leaving.

At the time, my daughter Imaara was a very small child and I was in love with her. My heart flew out my chest because I had to leave my daughter, and also knew I had no where to go. I wasn't scared; I was shocked at my reality. I had no family in New Jersey that I could confide in, or maybe just go to sleep in a fetal position on their couch. I had turned a new page in my book of life and the chapter began with, 'A gloomy and stormy night'... I was sad, very sad. For some reason in the middle of this pain, my survival instincts kicked in like I was downloading a hunting game into my system. However, this was the street version with no rules. Although my vision was dark, I found light in the fact that my street knowledge took the lead. My worried mind seemed to go asleep and I went into auto-pilot. Thanks God for that small moment of peace within the chaos of my new reality. A shift in thought rescued my sanity.

At the time, we were living in a place called Maple Gardens in Irvington, NJ. The complex was a place secured from a world of concrete and violence right outside its gates. I knew I was headed out there with full contact. The person I had grown into had to be sedated and my old 'self' rose like an erect pillar to hold up my sanity. I remember becoming excited in a strange way. That may have been the chemicals in my brain changing to respond to a disaster. I knew I was all I had, and felt that, "Do something," moment from the movie John Q. This was the part of the movie when Denzel's wife screamed at him to "Do something!" Their son in the movie needed a transplant and Denzel felt trapped. He eventually got a gun and shut the hospital down. Now I didn't get a gun, but I felt my spirit smack me straight across the face because of the weight it was about to carry. "Damn you", it shouted out to me with a lingering echo.

Street Knowledge: The power within

I left the apartment with blood on my hands, shed from a broken family. I had faith, great faith that I was favored by God and I would once again do the impossible of starting over from nothing. I put myself in harms way as most of us do at times, and it is our responsibility to get back up from these unimaginable places of ruins. As I exited the protected gates where I lived, I was immediately exposed to the concrete jungle. I was not driving because we had only one car, which meant I was total out in the open to the elements of the inner-city streets. The only assets I had were $60, street knowledge and a personality people seemed to love and enjoy. I figured my character would help make my $60 status appear to be more than what meets the eye. I was trained to walk like money, which would at least get me closer to an opportunity.

Drug-dealing wasn't an option; it was beneath me at this point. The thought of my children being left a legacy of their father being killed on the streets because of drug dealing, was just too inappropriate. Come on family, some things we really grow up out of, and drug-dealing were one of them.

My new frontier on the streets had me focused like a hawk looking for food. I was walking fast and thinking faster, with moments of talking to myself. My dress code those days had developed into a daily cool-casual look. At times people would say to me, "Why are you always dressed up?" I wasn't always dressed up; I was always ready to run into Russell Simmons or Oprah. This may seem far fetched, but you never knew. So that night as I strutted through the streets, people were looking with stares of confusion, as I had on a white tucked in t-shirt with blue blazer, jeans, stark white sneakers, and a clean shaved face. They didn't know if I was a police or politician trying to act normal and without fear.

I knew I had to move quickly while my look was still crispy clean. I walked over into Newark, which were only a few blocks away from that part of Newark. I went straight to a couple of Drug spots and looked for the guys that were making the most money on the scene. These guys knew me from my days of being someone who used to be one of them in my era. This is called street-credibility. I approached a few of these guys with my story of separation and need of a loan. These young soldiers gave off a sense that they were honored to help me. Most of them used to watch me from afar with admiration in the past during my days on the streets. Now that I turned my life around successfully from negative to positive, the respect seemed greater. I had street credibility. Many on the streets don't despise the "right way" of living; it is the major steps towards lifestyle change that appear so painful of a task.

I received some money from a few on the streets and believe me, it wasn't a huge amount. It was enough to take some anxiety off my neck. I was able to swallow again because my mouth was physically dry. My anxiety had lowered and my thoughts were able to focus on my great exit out of a hardship door. My present situation was difficult and disheartening, which was hard to shake off my spirit. I had to find a place of peace; somewhere I could be alone and out of the elements of the constant street noise. It felt like every loud siren carried a message to me about the emergency I had on my hands.

This time was especially rough because I was in between jobs, which means I had no job at the time. I was due to begin working in a new position within the next three weeks. Family, the struggling middle-class is not a myth, I've been living it. The idea of a household with an approximate $80,000 a year budget is basically for bills and gas. I could never save money, and I wasn't placing much effort into that much important aspect either. In those days, I was more focused on developing a solid career and being happy within the lifestyle change I was busy making a solid reality. I can't leave out the fact that I had three children at the time, so money was just to cover my basic needs. A saving account at the time was unfortunately not a part of my equation.

As I moved desperately through the streets, my thoughts were racing and reflecting on many things about my life. Although I've always worked to advance my career and did it with diligence, there was always a pull on my focus to be self-employed. Could I have advance educationally and been more secure with less distractions of business ventures? Could I have been in leadership positions by now? I've always had one eye on ways to get paid outside of the workforce. So my one foot in and one foot out, may have caused some delay in my professional gain. In life family, anything we do will take the focus off something else. Yes I took risks in my financial stability, but I'm extremely happy that my prior street lifestyle had no influence on my life. As long as my intentions were not invested in negative behaviors, I was living my mother's words, "There is only one way and that's the right way." There were many who have said I've wasted time with trying to start businesses and left my educational endeavors. These people were not there when I was sitting in a correctional facility with hopes that I would make it to be a man with just a new way of thinking. So theses thoughts were racing in my mind, which eventually led me back to a place where I thanked God for who I have become thus far.

I had no regrets about my new disposition as a homeless man in America. I had some education, good work ethics, faith in a higher power, and about three hundred dollars. There was faith more than anything because things were not looking and feeling good. I ended the night by catching the bus to the Rivera Hotel on Dr. Martin Luther King Boulevard in Newark. This is a hotel in one of the most drug-infested areas of the city. The hotel has been called a 'welfare hotel'. I didn't care, I grew up on welfare. I just needed to be alone and think about my next move and exit out of difficulty. I sat at the end of the bed and my constant thoughts of disbelief about my present position in life put me to sleep. There are times family, when comfort depends on your present place in life. I found that comfort, right there at this so-called 'welfare hotel'.

God give me a sign

I woke up that morning with the words 'relationships' on my spirit. I began to think of old relationships that could help me in my new dilemma. I jumped off the bed and shouted, "I got it!" You would have thought I hit the lottery. I did in my own world between those walls of the Rivera hotel. I began thinking about a landlord Ayesha and I had rented a house from in the past, in which I maintained a fairly good relationship. In fact, I had moved in the house from another building he owned. So we had a positive rental and relationship history. I immediately knew I needed to call him. I did not want to think about if I should do it or not, so I just called him and he picked up. Francis was his name and he was an older Italian gentleman, who was cool with an easy going spirit. He said, "Tyrone. How's the family?" I responded, "Not to good and I need a big favor." I went right into why I called and didn't allow anxiety and pressure to take over my words or focus. I asked, "Is the house we were renting from you still empty in Union, NJ?" He said, "Yes." I almost cried as I felt my voice began to crack from hope that the phone call was a good decision. I told him to hold on as I collected my breath and turned up the volume to my boldness. I continued to explain my story of separation and he empathized with me. I informed him that I had no place to go and needed somewhere to stay until I get back on my feet. I told him that I had little money but would be working in a few weeks. He asked do I have any money now to give him until I started working. I gave him one hundred of the three hundred dollars I had. Francis said, "Ok Tyrone, you are a stand up fellow. Sure, I will help you." We planned to meet that day and he hung up the phone. I cried tears of joy and pain.

This was one of those times where you know there had to be higher power. I began to stare at my hands and rubbing my arms, then looking into the mirror in front of me. I had feelings of gratefulness, excitement and pity for this 34 year-old man's complex life. I never wanted to live a life of barely escaping harm. That's not a life for no one to live. The blessings that saved me from complete homelessness also left feelings that challenged my self-worth. Who wants to live a life continually questioning their manhood and the ability to be a so-called "normal" dad? The kind of dad that didn't have all that extra stuff going on such as a broken home, no income, no place to stay and a confused mind. I didn't want that for my children and that's why it was so painful. I knew those who loved me would shed many tears because of what I have been through and now standing in a 'welfare hotel' room. Especially because of all the great efforts they knew I put into changing my life from negative to positive. I just stared at my blood-shot red eyes in the mirror from crying; wondering how is this going to end. As I left the room I looked back and said, "This is crazy." I pulled myself together and was ready to meet Francis.

I knew I had to shake the disbelief of being homeless because it wasn't helping at all, and plus I had a new situation on the table. I met with Francis and he expressed his trust and looked forward to helping me get back on my feet. He talked about how the house was getting work done on and some of the rooms where closed and I didn't have to pay anywhere near full rent. He insisted I save my money to move within a few months. Francis rescued me from a lot of talking mixed with pleading that I may have begun to do in the meeting. I've been known as a talker and I can only image the many words, concepts, ideas, and promises that would have come out of my mouth. There is nothing like watching a desperate man salivating from the mouth, it's disgusting. Francis chose to take the lead in the discussion, which kept me from possibly looking like a fool. Although I maintained good eye contact, I couldn't help but feel some shame. I was pleading to live in a place that was truly unfit and unsafe for living.

The meeting with Francis was about over then his last words were, "I don't know how long the lights will be on because the bill is not in my name. Unless you want to pay the $600 bill from the last person who lived here? So I don't know when they will turn the lights off." I responded with pure exhaustion in my tone, "We will discuss that when I call you." I had no more emotional energy at the time for a problem that was coming later. I couldn't stretch my mind to think of how I was going to get out of that when presently there was a crisis on my hands. I thanked Francis with a hug and promised to repay him as soon as possible. The promise I made to him was combined with my own dire need to get out of the wrecked reality.

Touchdown! That's how I felt as Francis closed the door behind him. I was in a familiar place and away from the street elements which can morph a person into the worst that's deep within them. I felt the negative walk and talk coming out of me as I was wondering the streets for that short period. I knew that one wrong turn on them streets could have a lasting affect on my life. Any trouble or brush with the law would have opened my past back up like a fresh wound. The years of hard work to change and make a better life would have been the past, and a criminal charge on any level would have become my new reality. For example, a run-in with a guy high on PCP; a robber that thinks I had money; drugs found by a cop and charged to me; protecting myself from harm; a stop and frisk that went wrong, or any scenario that you imagine can happen on them inner-city streets. My counseling certification and work history holds no weight in a crime-ridden city where the cops have to move fast and you have to respond exactly the way they want or you get laid down. Imagine me trying to explain to a police officer or detective that I just got separated and I've change my life, blah, blah, blah. That's how my words would have been sounding in slow motion as the cop who was responding to a 187 and pointed his gun yelling, "Everybody get down!" My thoughts were that you never know how it will go down in the city streets laced with crime. I was already down on my luck and knew it could get worst.

Now I was in a safe place in the town of Union sitting on a couch that was left by the previous tenet. I was in a psychologically safe place to plan. I looked around and the house was just not in good shape, which seemed to be a clear water reflection of my life. I got up off the couch and began to adapt into my new environment. This wasn't hard for me as it seemed my last name had become 'adaptation'. Tyrone Adaptation was me and it wasn't funny as it sounds. Who the heck wants to start all over again, after they have started all over again, and over again? Hey, I guess I could only thank God for another chance to start all over again. Someone once told me that if God gives you another day, it translates into another opportunity for great changes.

Weeks went by and I started my new job just at the right time. I had only fifty dollars left and felt that should get me to and from work until I get paycheck. I took a Senior Counselor position with a company I've worked for in the past. The good thing was that I was familiar with working with this organization, the staff, and most importantly the population we served. I took a position working back within the criminal justice system. This time it seemed so draining on my spirit and psyche. Being a helper is one thing, but the facility where I worked had approximately 600 men that I was exposed to daily. Their feelings, concerns and needs, on top of my issues felt so heavy this time around. I was good at my job duties because I'd worked in this environment for years, but I felt something in my gut that became more and more uncomfortable everyday I came to work.

Transformation: A cocoon story

I knew in the past I wanted to take my talents and move to a different population in Human Services, but didn't know exactly what at the time. I guess now that I was experiencing hardship in my personal life, I began to feel the need to better manage the direction of my career. I began to listen more closely to these thoughts and they where compounded by voices of the past insisting that I do more in my career. Those were the voices I was pushing out of my head, in order to listen to the voice within that had my signature on them. Who I am and what I was becoming needed to be signed and sealed by yours truly. This was a crucial time in my life when I was rebuilding and refocusing to get it right again. I had to move away from self-pity and feelings of doubt. At times when things don't work out right, you begin to think that you should have done something when others told you to do it. You know that noise within can be like a war within.

Family, I can tell you now that until you are truly ready to act on anything in life, it won't happen. People that don't respect the autonomy of others, or are not mindful in their approach in giving advice could be killing the spirit of the person "they" feel needs some changing. I read a story once that gives a great example of how pushing change on others can end with devastation. It went something like this:

There was a cocoon in its normal stage of transformation at the bottom of a tree. A person saw the cocoon and express interest in speeding the process of the cocoon into a butterfly. He used a device to blow hot air near the cocoon. This person watched in excitement as the butterfly quickly transformed. He then became confused and frustrated because the butterfly wings were crippled. The natural process of change was interrupted and forced.

I knew something great was happening in my spirit and was delighted that I was ready and not crippled by other's desire for me to, "Do something!" I prefer to move on that command when it's coming from me, which will create a space for the best results. This great something that was happening to me, began raising my level of awareness as well. This came in a form of listening closely to the God within.

One day walking through the halls of my job, I saw the Director who I share good communication with for years. Family, from out of nowhere I said to her "Can you be my professional mentor?" She looked at me like I had two heads on my shoulder. She like others knew me as someone who had it all figured out or just acted like I did. That day, it was evident that I didn't. She said, "Hartman you don't need a mentor. You need to stop playing and finally go back to school. I want to move you up to management but you only have a CADC (Certified Alcohol and Drug Counselor) certification and that doesn't allow me to do it. You are like one of the leaders around here, someone I know that can present themselves professionally. You conduct some of the best lectures in the building to the residents, but you need more education and credentials so we can move you to where you need to be." Now I was looking at her like she had two heads.

Her words were perfect timing and I was in a good spiritual place to receive a blessing. Sometimes we can miss our blessing because our minds and spirits are so clouded. The voice within let me know those were the words that I needed to hear, and the time was ripe. I responded quickly, "OK, I will do that because you're right and this conversation was not by chance. My life needs an upgrade more than you know. I'm going to put in an application down at Rutgers in Newark. I have about approximately 40 credits from Essex County College because I took all the required classes for my CADC at the college. I may be able to transfer those credits. I see the vision and I'm definitely on deck with this." She then responded in a calm tone, "Hartman you are a smart guy, but I need to tell you that you may want to attend the HBCU (Historically Black Colleges and Universities) Lincoln University. Come to my office so we can have a quick sit down. I'm going to kill you because you know I'm busy." She was actually a very busy woman and I felt a great sense of pride that she was making sure I was informed about a way to take my life to the next level.

I followed her to the office with my chest poked out just a little bit as others watched. A supervisor walking down the hall yelled, "What y'all up to?" He thought we were going to make a power move or something in that nature. He didn't know I was going in her office to be empowered. We sat down and she began, "OK Hartman let me tell you about an opportunity that is about to be shut down real soon, and it's been in existence for decades. I don't want you to waste your time at Rutgers because you are too advanced to go the tradition route at this time in your life. You need to move into the big leagues while the opportunity is still possible." I was feeling like we were in the underground slave railroad or some exclusive meeting. I was again, honored to be talking to her on this level, or at least she was talking to me. "This University has one program for Human Service workers that will take all of your professional work history and educational background into account for a spot in a Master's program. This is nothing new under the sun but since it's from a Black University and many are receiving there counseling license, they are about to shut it down. There is something in the world of education called the CLEP (College Level Examination Program) tests that people take to advance them through colleges. The tests are useful for students who have obtained knowledge outside the classroom." She paused for a moment and asked, "How many years do you have working in Human Services?" I said, "I have about nine years in right now." She began explaining again, "That's what they do right there. The University considers those years in the concentrated field of Human Services, with your present credentials, and then you take exams to qualify you to enroll in the Master's degree program. Please don't let the title Master's degree scare you either. I know you can do the work. Much will be required of you, but you're crazy like me." I had big respect for her abilities to be in a leadership role within this vast criminal justice population. I would be proud to walk the halls my Director had walked.

Taking the challenge

This was a next level conversation. In fact, I felt the level was a bit overwhelming. I did not imagine this kind of expectation would be put in my lap on that very day. She got up out of her chair and walked to pick up this large book. She said, "This is my thesis. I put the work in and I you will have to as well. I'm telling you Hartman that if you want to take your life to the next level, you better jump on the boat now. That CADC you have will turn into a LCADC which will be a Licensed Clinical Alcohol and Drug Counselor once you get your Master's degree. This may take you three years but it's worth every dime you will spend through financial aid. They are going to stop this program soon and it has been in existence for decades. The industry is changing and I've been told by powers that are in control over many educational systems, that there is a focus to take down this program. The next enrollment is this September and you better be on it. That's right boy you have less than five months before then and a few weeks to get on board with registration." I was looking at her speechless and she said, "Now get out of my office and you owe me. Now the people for accreditation are coming in next week to do an audit of the program and you will be one of the people I pick to be conducting a lecturer. So get ready for a long lecture. Bye Hartman." This woman kicked right back into business mode like we were not having one of those moments. Maybe that was just me in the moment. That was good stuff.

I was more than grateful for the talk I had with my Director. Family, there is a voice within that speaks to us and at times we may need to silence the noise within in order to receive a profound message. There could be a message to guide us to or from something that may save our lives. This is in the sense of being awake as we are living our dreams versus being asleep while we are awake. The desire we all share as humans is to belong to something. I had a deep desire to belong to something greater than myself. I want to be awake while my dreams are unfolding and streaming-live. I listened to that voice and silenced the noise. There is a book titled, "Stillness Speaks," and it discusses in great details about the stillness we may want to connect with more often than not. This will provide us with a more comprehensive way of viewing living. Whole living is to exercise all of our abilities to gain a prosperous life which includes: Emotional Riches, Mental Riches, Spiritual Riches, and Financial Riches. This Stillness will be the powerful asset that will change our personal language into rich words such as: Mindfulness, Relaxation, Quite Time and Peacefulness. I was listening and caught the message...I was in a great state of humility that day.

I left work that day feeling like Bruce Leroy from the movie "Last Dragon" when he had the GLOW. When thoughts are sparked and you have insight to a brighter and fulfilling future, it's a feeling that can put you into a zone. This mindset was unsettling because it felt active like a soda that was shaken. I felt like I was two people at one time because I vividly imagined doing and becoming greater. The feelings of having an idea or thought, and you know something good is about to happen. You just can't get it out of your mind. The anticipation of flourishing that won't let you go to sleep. The feelings that make you excited about waking up in the morning. The enthusiasm felt when something special is about to take off. The movie, "Pursuit of Happiness" played by Will Smith, captured that passion and vision of being and feeling valuable while you are moving towards those crystal clear goals. The 'you' that people don't even know of at the time. It's that smirk of confidence. Those are the moments when you feel rich. When you are Rich in spirit, the bank account is unlimited. At times, "Be Still" and let your spirit and deep emotions speak.

That day was particularly memorable because when I arrived back at my living quarters (abandon house), I was focused on putting some of those beautifully thoughts and ideas on paper. So I click the lights on, but nothing happened. I went into two different rooms and only got a click without lights. The lights were off at this place I began to identify as my 'hide away'. I didn't panic or flinch, not even for a second. The level of acceptance to my reality was in a good place. I played back the tape when Francis the landlord informed me that the lights were going to be shout off, which I actually thought was going to be sooner than it happened. That night though, I had the light within powerfully shining. There was nothing that could have taken that joy that day of great revelation. As I went to sleep, it was like I had a ball of light in the palm of my hand. Imagine glowing in the dark...that was me, E.T. the Extra Terrestrial.

Time past, I gratefully was able to finance a $3,200 hundred dollar car and move out of my homeless place of residence. That experience did not go without great psychological and emotional strife. There were things that I did to get through those harsh times that I can say were very unhealthy. The state of depression had me in some really tough places (mentally) many of those days. Depression sat on me and was hard to shake at times. I thank God for the spirit and character that I'm blessed to have as a part of my strengths. Depression can cause a person to become suicidal because of the lack of self-worth and sadness about one's reality. Depression can cause a person to drink alcohol every night just to go sleep. Depression can lead to unsafe sexual encounters due to chasing a false sense of reality. Depression can lead to isolation, which is very unhealthy way to live. Solitary confinement is the worst kind of punishment and depression had sentenced me to that kind of self-inflicted pain. Throughout many of those days, I was homeless physically and spiritually. Family, I took part on all of the above mentioned acts due to depression. I was a mess many of those days and only the great mind of optimism helped rescue a hopeless wrecked ship like me. I slowly came out of my depression over time and began repairing the damage. Many times I thank God for being alive with a sane mind.

So as months went by and I had this great 'light' within on, I fed off of the energy and lit other areas of my life. I was proactive about contacting Lincoln University to begin the process of going back to school. I fulfilled all of the requirements for enrollment and ultimately got accepted. I was extremely excited that I wasn't required to go through the Pre-Master's program. This was required if the school deemed an individual needed an academic upgrade before they enter the Master's program. That would have been another entire year. I was a little more than excited about that, I was elated. I know many who went through the Pre-Master's program and they expressed it was worth the time and money. I didn't know it then, but the work require for

Master's program needs great preparation. I, on the other hand, was lacking emotional readiness. An unhealthy emotional state can tear a beautiful well-intended experience to pieces. I wish there was a Pre-Emotional class. So I raised my awareness of what I was lacking and began to prepare myself emotionally. I was taken on this task with some major challenges at that time in my life

While my 'light' within was still brighter than ever, I used it to see what other areas I needed to release from my life. I was overwhelmed in the work I was doing within criminal justice aspect of Human Services, and it became emotionally exhausted. I knew this was a train wreck waiting to happen if I didn't get myself emotionally prepared. My job would not have been a 'good look' for me and my new marriage to education. We usually have to divorce something to benefit from another endeavor, and I made the decision to move away from working with that population. I used the energy from the 'light' within while it was flaming hot. Family, you know at times that light can go dim and I wanted to exhaust every bit of it while I it was lit.

America: "The United States of Amnesia"

I call America, "The United States of Amnesia," because we forget on many occasions the things in our lives we need to truly stay mindful about most of the time. Distractions comes in all shapes and sizes, which my job at the time fit the description of being a full-blow distraction. Thank you 'light' within, I listened. However, the million dollar question was: Where and what kind of work do I want to do? I went into a brainstorm mode for about three days. My mind was speeding with thoughts and I came out of the three day focus with the idea of the Psychiatric population. I figured working within the fast-pace of the criminal-justice environment for approximately 10 years I have the capabilities and energy to merge into that line of work. I told myself to just do it, and do it boldly.

At the time of this job change, my salary was about $42,000 a year. I was a Certified Alcohol and Drug Counselor, which was a relevant credential in the field of Psychiatry as I grew to understand. So I resigned from my job and took a position as a Mental Health Tech at Summit Oaks Psychiatric Hospital. Why was this move a particular bold one? Family, my salary was reduced to about $25,000 a year. Ouch! I needed to change the burning gear that I felt within my spirit because it was wearing me down. So I made the switch, along with the salary decrease. I felt this move was very purposeful. There is a saying: "Take one step back, in order to take two steps forward." The quote was my mighty helmet that protected the inevitable distractive thoughts from entering my mind.

This salary drop took place because I was occupying a position of someone who aides the counselors, therapist, psychiatrist and other key roles in the facility. There was one Certified Alcohol and Drug Counselor in the hospital, which made the kind of salary that I chose to move away from with a purpose. I've had personal Case-Aides throughout my career and this positioned me in a state of humility. I fully accepted the status quo change that was coming down the pike. This was a recognize sacrifice that had some people scratching their heads at my decision. I knew what I was doing and besides, I was listening to 'light' within. I began to trust myself again and I wasn't allowing my thoughts to move in the direction of doubt.

Psychiatry was a new and interesting world that opened my mind and expanded my worldview. The type of patients we served had an array of disorders such as Schizophrenia, Bi-Polar, Major Depression and Substance Abuse disorders to name a few. In fact, there is an entire book of disorders and the specific details for diagnosing. The DSM-Diagnostic Statistical Manual is the Bible of Psychiatry. Psychiatrist, Doctors, counselors and mental health works all refer to this manual professionally. This book has every disorder you could think of and more.

I was enjoying learning something new and felt privileged to be exposed to a different path that many traditional Certified Alcohol and Drug Counselor's were not embarking on at the time. I not only adapted in the environment, I knew I wanted to stay in Psychiatry for a long time. Making a move from one type of career work to another can be challenging and scary at times. I didn't know what was going to be the results but I just stepped out on faith. Family, there are those times in life when we just have to trust in our abilities, strengths and vision.

So now I'm just all brand new and feeling good about my direction. I was in a different work setting, with a new school endeavor leading towards a more advanced individual. The school adventure was more than I expected though. The Master's degree program and I did fit like a hand and glove, and that's because I made it work. I always wanted to know more educationally, and it was happening. Lincoln University's curriculum for the program had an amazing flow, which help to ease the 20 page papers that I had to write. My first set of classes consisted of: Systems Theory, Ethics, Psychology and a Field class. I enjoyed how the curriculum seemed to make the learning experience a personal journey. As an adult learners, I have to be truly interested in the education I invest my time and money. When you are an older-adult, there is little room to make many major changes like a 21-year old student. The Lincoln experience kicked off to a great start.

I was intrigued by some of the assignments at the beginning of this educational journey. In my Field class, we were given the task of developing a Professional Portfolio. I had to gather any and all letters, certificates, awards, prior school work and other professional and educational related documents. All this information was collected from old folders and dusty bins I've had for years. These many different documents were all placed in a huge binder and my professional history just unfolded. I had forgotten about some of the things I've done in my career that were significant to my growth. The portfolio was also very therapeutic for me because it caused me to reflect on the trials and success I've encountered. In there I put the Real Estate License appeal letter I when I had to battle the commission to let me receive my license. The work I'd done to obtain my CADC certification was placed in the binder with pride. Also the two 'Employee of the Month' awards I received over the years. I had to write an introduction for this assignment along with some other specific details, which led to the Professional Portfolio. This was an instant upgrade for me because I never had or thought of such a portfolio. Although there were many other topics covered in the course, this gave me an impression the school had a great interested in the student's growth. The stage was set just right, and I was most grateful for the opportunity.

Divorce: A life changing event

The demands and joys of the school did not stop all the life's boulders of stress from being released. Ayesha and I decided to stay married and gave it another try at raising our daughter together. However while I was in school we separated again, and this time it resulted in divorce. Yes family, the big "D" word. This time was different though because on my birthday, October 28, 2008, the greatest gift ever was the birth of Adam on my B-day. This big curly afro boy was a priceless B-day gift from God. I thought having a child would be another form of glue that sealed our relationship, but it didn't work. I was very saddened by that because we are great parents and it was proven through the great work we put into our daughter Imaara's development.

Stress and depression was beginning to rock the boat, but I began to focus more on school and work. I knew what would be the results if I gave the depression any more of my attention. Thoughts of worthlessness were creeping on me and I had to shake it. I mean, there I was with two sets of children by two women and the relationships were not that great. My thoughts raced of being a Black man in America with more children unattended and without a father in the household. That was a stereotype I struggled very hard with at the time. Those were the heavy weighing conversations I was having daily. I pushed hard though, towards being optimistic about a better tomorrow.

Everything I've done has always been to be a better father. When I learn more, I have more to teach. The more money

I make, the more smiles from satisfying my children's needs and desires. My drive to never give up in life is an example that I pass to them. My experience as a father has been met with many struggles. I have always been a passionate man and father, which kept my head up high. Who I am as a man and father is what helped me move away from depression. I had to give attention to the many good thoughts of my fatherhood. I had to pull out the many 'Thank you' letters from all of my children's schools for great parent participation. I tell you, there's nothing like having physical proof of the work I've put in their lives, because I needed it during those trying times. The song "I reminisce, I reminisce," by rapper CL Smooth was my theme song during those times. I was even thinking about writing a book titled, "Poppa Wasn't a Rolling Stone, We Just Didn't Get Along." Who wants to be a part of negative stereotypes? Not me! I struggled with that for a long time, and still get negative feelings about not being a part of that two parent home set-up.

The birth of Adam was very special to me and not just because he was born on my birthday. You see, my son Tyrone was born 1 pound and 7 ounce with complications that didn't allow him do the many activities that boys normally wrestled. You know the running, jumping, and wild but expected actions of a boy exploring the land. Tyrone has his own unique space, which are the extraordinary blessings God placed on his life that allowed him to be living for me and his mother Eris to enjoy. His huge personality is a reflection of living life and not just existing. Tyrone's presence is one of strength and hope. The greatest gift is when your son wants to be like you, and Tyrone has begun his plight to be a great man. Many people say he's very talkative like me, and I guess I can confirm that observation. His favorite words have come to be, "Let me talk to you for a minute." Then he, like me, will put you in a spider web of conversation. Got you!

Adam was just a brand new baby and it was emotional for me at the time. Ayesha and I had recently gotten a divorce, and he was so innocent to all the mess that I was working to recover from in order to get my life back. It caused me great sadness that I was not going to be able to change his pampers at night, as I did Tyrone's. I did know he was going to be my outgoing boy. He is a child I watch in admiration as he jump from slides at the park instead of properly sliding. I knew he was going to love his dad, which provided me with another opportunity to live. Tyrone was going to be able to watch his brother be active and also live again. Although I was not comfortable with some things in my life, I had many things that revealed I was being blessed. Family, I had to take the focus off what's wrong with my live, and took time to be grateful.

Although the stressors were there, I continued with the 'end in mind'. The end being the benefits of me obtaining my Master's degree. I knew my professional credential CADC would turn into a LCADC. This would automatically place me on a supervisory level because CADC holders were supervised by LCADC. I would be identified as an expert in the field of Substance Abuse Counselor. I would be at the top of my 'game' in a field that I endured many professional war scars. So I kept all these motivating factors in the front part of my brain. This was how I got through the constant strife. If I didn't have strong faith and a positive attitude, I would have ended up in the emergency room or some unpleasant place due to depression. I kept the faith and moved with an "S" on my chest towards graduation.

Yes family, I did it! I graduated from Lincoln University with a Master's in Human Services with a concentration in Counseling. I could not have done it without some of the positive support of my fellow classmates and the great professors at Lincoln University's Graduate program at the Philadelphia campus. Oh', I forget to mention that I traveled to Philly every week. Translation, more stress. I didn't even want to mention that because of the stress that may have crept through my fingertips as I typed. The educational journey was not only worth it, I truly learned a lot about myself and others. I learned much about organizational systems from Professor Wortz. I learned the next level of Psychology and Human Development from Dr. Price. I learn from Dr. Plantz, the great benefits of functioning from the "WE" and not the "I", which is the Westernized way of thinking and being. Rest in peace to Dr. Plantz, she was a class act.

Today was a good day

My graduation was held at the main campus where the young and hopeful teenagers dwelled down in Lincoln University, PA. The keynote speaker was a graduate from the Master's of Human Services program. He was the Commissioner of Philadelphia's Fire Department. He delivered an impactful motivational speech. He was a captivating speaker with a powerful message of hope. That was one of those "Yes we can" speeches that President Obama have people crying and carrying on emotionally. All my fellow graduates were beautiful. I didn't sense an ounce of negative energy. As Ice Cube said, "Today was a good day."

The greatest part of my graduation was the presence of my family. I asked Ayesha would she bring my children and she agreed. That meant a lot to me because our relationship had some challenges at the time. My oldest son Tyrone was present along with my dear mother. My mother was so proud of me because she knew more than anybody that all I want to do is to take care of all my love ones financially. My mother knew I had a passion for learning and now it was proven. My children got the chance to witness me graduate, which represented my respect for education. They need to know education is very important. I love to make statements that my children could benefit from and my graduation was a great example for them to follow. This was a perfect picture moment in history.

Now that I was a recent graduate, it was time for a different kind of discussions with employers. I had focused my energy throughout school by taking a lower paying position and that came with great sacrifice. I chose to do that and not become overwhelmed, which got me ready for what God had planned. I tell you family, I had high hopes for my career advancement. I was ready to let education work for me and benefit from the fruits of my labor.

Although my educational level had grew, my sense of self-worth and standards also reached new heights. The hard work we put in to making a change and taking our lives in a more responsible direction should never be taken lightly. I was in a posture of humility for almost three years being a Case-Aide, when I could have been a primary counselor. This spoke in volumes. No one owed me anything, but I owed it to myself to reach for the best possible opportunity.

My job search was more focused on leadership positions in Behavioral Health organizations. I wanted to help develop and train other staff members that were working within Human Services. I knew many of those I've worked with throughout the years could have used some good training material and an excellent trainer. Throughout my experience in school, I had to conduct many Power Point presentations. I had to do research about particular topics and organize the information into a thorough presentation. I actually began enjoying the idea of conducting these presentations in front of my fellow classmates. I also was used to doing lectures for about 100 men at a time in the criminal justice system. However, in class I was speaking to other professionals. The feeling was different and felt I would really enjoy having a career where I could work with the element of staff development. So, that was my objective and I wasn't bending.

The agency where I worked at the time knew the sacrifice I had made was about over and how my professional life was about to change. I put my application in to upgrade my New Jersey Certified Alcohol and Drug Counselor status to a Licensed Clinical Alcohol and Drug Counselor, and within weeks it arrived in the mail. I had a Master's degree and a counseling license, which immediately raised my value in the field of Human Services. There was constant talk of whether I was going to leave the organization or move to a higher position. These closed doors discussions became louder and louder. One day a clinical manager said, "Tyrone, what are going to do since you got all your credentials?" This was strange because we never really talked and she was kind of stand-offish. I said, "Well, I am interested in a Training position with the organization." She responded, "We don't have that position anymore." In my mind I said, "Well make one." That was funny. So I responded, "I'm just going to see what my options are out there in the field. I want to help develop staff members." She said, "You just going to use us until you find another job, huh? I quickly responded, "I have been given my best work on this Detox unit and I will continue to do the same." I walked away thinking how inappropriate she presented herself in that short meeting. Sometimes I think about how people just say what they want to say to others. That's what I'm talking about family, if your standards are not in tact, people will try to withdraw from your bank account of self-worth.

Raising the Bar

I began to put out my updated and polished resume in the market for positions such as Director, Manager, but mostly Trainer and Facilitator. This process of sending resume's out lasted for about three months and I began to notice doubt from others about my career direction. I remember the Rapper T-I had a song out with a hook that said, "You might see me on the street, but Homie you don't know me." See, that was my thinking as the vulture spirits began to loom. I used to say to myself, "We might work at the same job, but Homie you don't know me." I throw doubt right back in with the fish. Family, the education doesn't make us; it packages us better for what's to come in life. I didn't have entitlement issues, however I knew my character was that of a go-getter, and I wasn't letting up on my faith. My co-workers didn't know where my drive or great level of motivation. I came from the streets and my level of endurance was a little different from those I worked with. They figured I was a regular guy with big hopes. My co-workers didn't know the type of lifestyle I've come from or any of my trials. Family, never let people's thoughts of you take you off of your square. You don't want to become a puppet and move away from your plans too soon.

One day I got a phone call and the woman on the other end said, "Hello, may I speak to Tyrone Hartman. I responded, "Yes, this is me." She continued, "I have a position in the Psychiatric Emergency Room and we need someone with your credentials. You will not be working directly with patients. You would be training and educating staff. Is that ok with you? I did the Victor Cruz dance from the Giants before

I answered, "No that's not a problem because I have been looking for a Training and Educating position." After the conversation, we set up the date and I was ready to exercise my interviewing muscles. This was a great opportunity and she mentioned my history of working in psychiatry was an asset. My career navigation was making sense and dots were connecting.

The day of the interview came and I went as if the job belonged to me. I heard T.D Jakes say in his strong conviction, "You have to claim what you want." I did that and also used every drop of professional and clinical talk that I had hidden in my DNA. I focused on discussing the requirements of the job and made sure to stay away from salivating from the mouth. A wise man told me once, "People can sense your desperation and the best thing to do is to stay cool and focus on the topic, not the results." I did that and listened to T.D. Jakes. Those ingredients worked and I got the job. Thank you T.D Jakes, you were speaking to me.

The position was for a Co-occurring Specialist at the Jersey City Medical Center. They were looking to hire a professional who has the ability to work with clients who has been diagnosed with a Mental and Substance Abuse disorder. These individuals have these disorders at the same time of each other. The other name it's known by is MICA, which stands for Mentally Ill and Chemical Abuser. My responsibilities were to work directly with staff members in a Psychiatric Emergency Room, also known as a Screening Center. This was a place next to the regular ER-Emergency Room. The Psych ER is a place where someone may be in danger of themselves or others would be assessed by clinicians for psychiatric care. These individuals are brought in and may be committed into the Psych Ward in the hospital. These people come by way of their family members, police officers, ambulance workers, or even the individual may feel they want to commit suicide and just come in for psychiatric emergency services.

My position would be to train staff on the industries best practices when working with patients who are diagnosed with a Mental and Substance Abuse disorder. These consumers were unique to deal with because of the seriousness of the problems that can result from having both disorders. The use of drugs complicates the treatment of a person's Bipolar, Schizophrenia, or other disorders. I was also there to build education and resources for the Screeners, who were the clinicians. This was necessary because the workers were extremely busy and needed the support of someone to have material prepared for patients when they are discharged. I also was required to conduct trainings and consult with other staff members throughout the Behavioral Health system of the hospital. This included staff from around the hospital such as: the Psych ward, Detox Unit, Intensive Case Management Service workers, Children's unit, and other departments. This also included Psychiatrist and the nursing staff.

When I started working, I hit the ground running and was comfortable in the position because I fulfilled the job requirements. This was not because I knew someone or they needed someone to just fill the position. The hired person needed the counseling license I had, and no one in the Psych ER had my credentials. This validated me as an expert and I consulted with staff as such. However, as I worked there and recognized I was consulting with high functioning professionals, I felt a need for more education in the area of communication. I wanted to be equipped not only with consulting with people, but also with more impactful engagement.

I spoke to a friend of mine James Abiola (shout out) from Philadelphia about my thoughts of more education, and he led me to a school on the internet. The school he put me down on was Fielding's Graduate University. The school only offered Master's and Doctorate degrees. There was a Master's degree that caught my eye, which was in OMD-Organizational Management and Development, with a concentration in Coaching. I focused in on the Coaching aspect and felt this would be a great asset when communicating and consulting with staff members. I trusted my gut feelings and turned another educational page. A man has to do, what a man has to do…

Education: You can never go wrong

My life's stability was my primary focus. Hey, I couldn't let some success be my demise. That was my big past mistake. That was past damage. I knew there was more God had in store. So I applied and got accepted, after an intense application process. The application requirements almost caused me not to apply. I didn't feel like proving myself to anyone again about me being worthy to get on their boat. Those kind of negative feelings can creep up on you and cause some mental blockage. I had to shake that so I could move away from the spirit of 'poor me'. I wrote the necessary papers, collected recommendations, sent out for transcripts and fulfilled the many other requirements on the-to-do list. The process kind of flowed smoothly because I'd become accustom to filling out and satisfying so many requirements in an effort to not allow my criminal record of the past to slow me down. You see, the more skills, education and productivity one gains, the more they move further away from a challenging past that might affect an individual's job-life. My mother and I shared a saying, "keep it moving," and that played in my head at the right times. A good saying or words of encouragement can lift your spirits and it did for this latest educational installment. The need for motivation is up there with H2o. Tupac said, "You got to keep your head up."

I felt the upgrade in my life immediately as I entered the program with my online classmates. This was very interesting to me because I recently had a classroom educational experience, and now I was communicating with others online. The experience did provide me with a sense of being a part of an advance quest to obtain information. These people were serious about being online learning. The program provided me with a culture shock too. I had come from functioning at a Historically Black University, and now I'm the only brown dude in the class. I knew this was going to be an enlightening experience. I had the opportunity to widen my worldview again from interacting with various groups of people from around the country and Canada. This kind of relationship would probably never have taken place on such a large scale. The great opportunity was not only in working with a different group of people; it was the benefits of obtaining different new perspectives.

I began with the Coaching curriculum and was amazed by the learning that took place between the students, professors, and the material. The art of Coaching opened me up to an entire new way of assisting others in solve their own problems. I couldn't help but think of my long life as a counselor and all the work I was doing by talking people's head off. I was good at what did, but Coaching gave me some new lenses to look through. For example, I learned that when practitioner's talked less in a coaching session, there is more learning taking place. The primary focus in Coaching is that people know their own story and have solutions to the problems in their lives. There were concepts and models such as Mindfulness, Appreciative Inquiry, Positive Psychology, and other models that I was fortunate enough to learn. Lincoln University empowered me and sent me into the world a Master of Human Services, and my new educational experience opened up the doors of mainstream with a bulldozer.

Family, we have to keep pushing the envelope because our next level experience is waiting to take us to greatness.

My daily work schedule at the hospital consisted of traveling a lot throughout the building from department to department in order to train staff. One day as I was weaving through people saying hello to everyone and I saw a woman with a very vibrant face and smile. She caught my eye and I said, "Hello." I couldn't go any further because I worked with many departments and didn't want to cross any lines. She then said, "Hello, I see you all the time around the building, what do you do?" This was my turn to toot my own horn (we have to impress the ladies fellows), "I work directly with staff through training and consulting about evidence-based practices when they are working with patients. I may be doing some training on your unit sooner or later. I'm about to head out to California in a few days, so I will check my agenda when I get back." She responded with excitement, "OK! What are you going to Cali for? It is business or pleasure." I responded, "I'm going for business, but you can't help but enjoy Cali."

Yes, the needed trip. Family, I had a ball. This was the unexpected and great part of my second Master's program. The students had to meet for several days for an intense face to face coaching session. This took place in the beautiful Santa Barbara, California, which I stayed for a week. This trip was like the graduation present I never received when I graduated from Lincoln University. Also, I needed a vacation so badly. I wish I could scream through these pages to express my level of excitement and aliveness I felt about finally traveling after the many storms had past. My entrance into Fielding Graduate University's online program was a significant and life changing event.

The job was going well and my educational experience began shining new light on working in organizations. I think the light had gotten a little too bright. Family, after working for the hospital for approximately two years I began to want something different. I felt my work there was done. My career direction was on deck by working in psychiatry and becoming a trainer, which were my goals. I began to feel the people I was doing the trainings for were not enthusiastic as I imagined. I conducted well-informed trainings and had evaluations to prove it. However the culture of Human Services has become one that the focus is just keeping up with the paperwork. I've been a counselor/case manager for over a decade, and understood the anxieties caused when the pressure of supervisors, managers, directors, and client's charts are on your neck. So I was not disregarding the strains and demands of those I was conducting training for, I just knew there was a serious need for better client care. My focus in my Master's degree project at Lincoln University was on burnout in Human Services. So, I knew firsthand what takes place, as it pertains to the stress associated with working in Human Services. Nevertheless, my views were changing about the field I worked.

The mind: It wants more

My new educational investment was focused on Organizational development and management. This provided me with more insight about how organizations are even less concerned about the well-being of their employees. The research I conducted at Lincoln University on burnout was now making more sense. The study of organizational systems is very enlightening because organizations are a normal part of society. They are everywhere you look: businesses, churches, banks, schools, colleges, Unions, FEDS, politics, etc. So the next time you walk into any building, know that an organization has planned and is managing everything down to how many times they clean the bathroom a day.

I eventually became less interested in my position at the hospital and felt it was time for me to move in a different direction. I applied for another job position in the hospital that would put me closer to the organizational development team. I had a desire to make greater changes that are at the core of organizations. In this change I was trying to make, I even began sharing with some of the staff in the Psych ER of this new direction. I was not happy with my position anymore and knew I needed a change. I was at a place in my life where I knew I've work hard and deserved to be the most effective captain of my ship possible, and not just stay uncomfortable. The idea of pushing it to the limit is nothing new. I am American made. We all deserve more and should go after it in full effect. Something happen though, the noise in my head of discomfort was getting louder. The war within was a fight for freedom versus complacency. I was earning a good salary and change is an unknown venture at times. So I figured I would ride it out for a while.

My small relationship with Fatima had turned into a date. I'm happy we went out because a brother needs to know he still got it. I took her to go shoot pool over in Hoboken, which was different and fun. Then I drove over to Jersey City by the Hudson River for a nice dinner. We talked extensive about many common interests we shared. We both were from Newark and not the best areas. We both worked in Human Service for many years, and enjoyed assisting others in their growth process. We both worked for criminal justice model facility at different times. We talked about music and how back in the day Hip-Hop was the best ever. We agreed the music back in the late 80's and early 90's was true soul music. The conversation went on like we were old friends. At the end of the time we spent, I said, "We are from the same tribe, I'm glad we came." The date was like a breath of fresh air with a lot of laughter.

The hardships of past relationships can feel like it's not even worth getting serious anymore. The possibility of love is always an option. We have to pay close attention to how much our trust issues are going to get in the way of growing a new relationship. First we have to except that we have trust issues. I tell you, if you have ever been lied to, hurt, or a relationship didn't go your way, then you are a candidate for trust issue. I'm not being negative about having trust issues; I'm saying that trust issues negatively affected me and others I know. My point is to share how one's past can get in the way of love. I think I'm going to try love again.

I woke up the next day with my spirit feeling strange. My mind took me to a place where once someone said to me,

"Hartman, the bigger you are, the harder you fall." That thought stuck out to me as I dressed and went to work. I didn't know it at the time, but my behavior had become careless at the job. I lost the enthusiastic personality people looked forward to when I entered different departments. I was less genuine and it showed. I remember clearly now how people use to say, "Tyrone is everything ok. Where's the motivation that you always talk about." The noise inside my head was too loud to respond properly. I became unaware of the great level of dissatisfaction I was feeling at my workplace. I was suffering from the United States of Amnesia. I forgot what I needed to remember about directly my life. I forgot that pain and discomfort in the spirit has to be addressed and not disregarded. I tell you Family, if you don't make the changes that's needed, God will make them for you. In the words of Donald Trump on his Apprentice show, "You are FIRED!" That was me getting fired for the first time in my life. Ouch! That was a unique day to say the least. At least I had a hot date the night before. Sheesh, I was about tired of these ups and downs. Family, I guess that's what life's all about? The saying goes, "God doesn't put anything on us that we can't handle." At the time I was saying to God, "Really God…?"

Life: We fall down, but we get

I've talked about listening to that God voice within, which at times we miss. I missed it that morning before I got fired. I knew I should have left that job back when my spirit was expressing discomfort. I did apply for a different position and stopped when I got no respond. That's an example of not being pro-active or resourceful. I ended up tarnishing my career track record, but I was in a fog. I was in something called an unhealthy state of auto-pilot, which takes you further away from your conscious-self. The mode of job auto-pilot is concerned with nothing but work and more work. I was not in a totally dead state of mind; I was just in the United States of Amnesia. I had forgotten about the 'ME' that had developed a good sense of direction in life. We all loose ourselves at times. I guess the game is to lessen the risk factors of failure. The 'imperfect human' has a way of revealing how that notion is so perfectly true.

What's a brother to do at this point? I thought about how most people would be on edge about getting fired. I work in Psychiatry and I know getting fired can be anxiety producing. Although I got fired, I was able to get some of my conscious mind back in order to plan out how I was going to repackage my life. This was a very important lesson for me at the time. My new package was not to just get another job, but to get a life. A life that was more fulfilling. My life has consisted of education, work, education, and more work. Life has to be lived with a greater purpose. The hard work and dedication I put into building my life was an example that I had the tools to take my life to another level. I knew it was time to combine my education and work history with a vision for building an enterprise. I felt it was time to use my abilities to speak to people and with audiences on to a larger scale. There is a wealthy and passionate gentleman named Anthony Robbins, who said, "It is amazing what you can do in a decade." Being successful in anything doesn't happen overnight. I know the same patience and diligence I put into school and work, is the kind of energy necessary for building a business or enterprise. Entrepreneurship and my education is a wonderful marriage that I plan to arrange.

Bills have to be paid, so I began to apply for jobs carefully of my choice. I understood that when you need a paycheck and the wrong job calls you back, it becomes the right job. I felt like the game of working for these Human Services organization had become an unfriendly environment. My job search had very little of those agencies I was used to working, even though I loved working with the people we served. However, I think the pressures of Medicaid and insurance on the 'Helper' organizations is driving staff members up the wall. I've climbed enough and my rope was getting shorter with tolerance.

The calls and job interviews started coming in and one of them caught my attention. I had a small phone interview and received some e-mails from this organization, which made me feel things may go down the right way and I may get hired. As the process was moving, I began to think about how no matter the level of work or education I put in to my development, the anxiety of getting a background check always creeps in my skin. Again, I've battled the Real-Estate commission and NJ Consumer Affairs and won the privilege to be apart of these professional industries, but my record is always there in my head. I was 18 years-old when I went to the correctional facility, which was approximately 20 years ago. I still feel something negative when I apply for jobs, as it pertains to my past. To rent an apartment these days, a criminal background check is conducted. I know many people that feel they can never get ahead because of this and I'm here to scream, "KEEP IT MOVING!" The minute you stop putting in the efforts to move more towards being a productive member in society, the odds become greater against you at that point. Imagine if I would have stopped my efforts to be more; I would really be behind the eight ball of life. A big part of my motivation has always been to 'bring one home for the team'. My purpose in life has always been connected to being a positive role model to many. I know we have much to offer and we have to give much of ourselves to keep pushing towards our best self.

Family, I got the job and I was humbled for this great opportunity. I told the people in my life and they were excited. My mother was over-excited and I joked about her lost of words. I texted my partner Arthur Townes, who is now the Director of Alumni for a huge Human Service organization (shout out), and he called me back just to make sure he got the text correctly. I know it wasn't the job itself they were excited about; it was that they knew I wanted to be apart of something bigger than myself. They knew I loved people and never would stop until I was able to express that love to as many people possible. Love is more powerful than we acknowledge at times.

I entered the room, wrote my name on the board and said, "You can call me Professor Hartman, I will be instructing this course." Family, life can be like a wild horse that needs patience and good practice to ride it. Hold on tight. You are up next...

Part Three

WORDS OF MOTIVATION

ABLE

You are able to bring those hard-hitting results into your life. The goals and aspirations you have are on a standstill until you proactively begin to work towards fulfilling them. Things happen twice: first in the mind, then in the physical. Think big and do big things. Your powerful abilities will enable you to put your all into your dreams like never before. Because today, you are in a zone that will help you key in on what you are capable of achieving. Now Get busy!

■ How can this word be applied to your life?

■ How can this word be applied to your family and community?

You are able to be a winner by investing the right kind of energy into your plans.

ACCEPT

There will be times in life when you will have to accept something that may be painful or uncomfortable. This act of acceptance will only make you stronger and more confident in the decisions you make. You will be especially focused on what you can change at the time. Accept whom you are and where you are in life, in order to get to the beautiful you. Right now, you may be at the caterpillar stage in life, but you will transform into that beautiful butterfly. Let it go and you will grow.

■ How can this word be applied to your life?

■ How can this word be applied to your family and community?

Accept and welcome your responsibilities.

ACCOMPLISH

You have the ability to accomplish your wildest dreams and make a contribution to the world. Live in the spirit of your last accomplishment, it causes a winning attitude. Take every accomplishment serious because you will have to repeat that winning mind-set in your life's journey. The chance for you to become an asset to the world is waiting for your innovation to produce. Lets' make it happen!

■ How can this word be applied to your life?

■ How can this word be applied to your family and community?

What dream would you like to accomplish?

ACHIEVE

Imagine if you made it happen and financial freedom was at your fingertips. Wow! Achieving that high level of economical success will take a great sense of passion. A friend once told me, "There's no time to bleed." He was expressing that in route to achieving your glory, there is no time for complaining, kicking, screaming, and putting doubt on your abilities. So what if you've made mistakes, bad decisions, or have a speech impediment? Big deal if you have a weight problem, or some character defects. It doesn't matter anymore. Today is the day to say, "I know I can, be what I want to be."

■ How can this word be applied to your life?

■ How can this word be applied to your family and community?

Achieving goals is one of the greatest feelings ever.

ACQUIRE

Acquire a desire to diversify your social portfolio. Go ahead and meet new people from different cultures. This can only add to your personality and provide you with a strong sense of open-mindedness. Try new foods and stimulate your taste buds. Turn your next vacation into a cultural learning experience. Read up on other people's nationalities and how they operate in their communities. Get yourself prepared and equipped for the new world of diversity. It's going to be empowering.

■ How can this word be applied to your life?

■ How can this word be applied to your family and community?

Acquire higher learning and then reap the benefits.

ACTIVE

No matter how it takes place, you will continue to develop into someone different than who you are today. Change is inevitable, it will happen whether it advances your life or puts you knee deep into difficulty. When you're not active and taking full responsibility for your personal growth, it's like living life as a fool in hope. Some feel luck is good enough. I don't think so! You will want to be an active participate in that change process. Be the main actor or actress in your life and let the cameras roll. You are the next blockbuster hit!

■ How can this word be applied to your life?

■ How can this word be applied to your family and community?

Be an active member in your family and community.

ADVANCE

As you advance in life, there will be negative people and roadblocks. The harmful energies that people pass on have the ability to infect your life and poison your thought patterns. This can pass on the germs that will spread like a wild fire on your spirit. This will contaminate your good value system with polluted beliefs. But, the good thing about life is that there is something called balance. Life offers just as many good spirited and extraordinary people, and you will need to steer in their direction. Locate as much positive light as possible, because your life will always be tested.

■ How can this word be applied to your life?

■ How can this word be applied to your family and community?

Advance to the level of presidential status.

AFFECT

Did you know there was a difference between your feelings and emotions? They are related to one another like first cousins however one comes before the other. For example: If a friend speaks to you in a way that you don't like or appreciate—the first thing that happens is you will "feel" the effects of it. The "emotions" come into play, when you keep playing what happened in your head like an old rerun of the Cosby show. Now you can't seem to get it out of your mind. The longer you decide to let it rent space in your head, the more frustrated you will become. So I suggest once you feel the negative feeling of a person or situation, address it ASAP (as soon as possible). Then have a good day.

■ How can this word be applied to your life?

____

____

____

____

____

____

■ How can this word be applied to your family and community?

____

____

____

____

____

____

Negative thoughts will affect the way you talk and act towards others. Get them off you spirit sooner than later.

AFFIRM

Whether you're aware of it or not, you are influenced by the people around you. This can be proven by closely evaluating your associates, friends, and family members. These people have strengths and weaknesses that you can either accept or reject when you're interacting with them. Think about those in your life who are powerful and those who have ugly habits. Affirm the characteristics that are more useful and attractive to you. Let it be known that you desire the best in others.

■ How can this word be applied to your life?

■ How can this word be applied to your family and community?

Affirm the beliefs and principles that make you a smart and good-spirited person.

AGREE

When you're coming to an agreement and resolving a problem or issue, it will be a satisfying relief. It's a good thing to take on a new idea and step out of your stubbornness, in order to do what is right. That ego of yours can be as big as the Trump Towers. However, if not balanced correctly it can get in the way and delay your upward mobility in life. Once that ego steps in, rationality usually steps out. Free your mind from what others may think of you and continue to reinvent yourself. Agree to a better way of doing things.

■ How can this word be applied to your life?

■ How can this word be applied to your family and community?

Agree to what is best and ignore your emotional thinking.

ALERT

Turn your energy level up and stop wasting time. You know society will eat you up and spit you out. Are you dragging your feet and procrastinating? Get up, get out, and do something. Don't let your whole life pass you by. Alertness breeds people that are ready for opportunities. It also prepares those who have faith and are consciously walking towards their future. Stay alert of the blessings that are near and don't give up too soon.

■ How can this word be applied to your life?

■ How can this word be applied to your family and community?

Be alert at all times and be mindful of your surroundings.

ALIVE

Live life, don't just exist. Bring that leader alive that's within. Volunteer your services, invest in people, and enlighten others. You will feel alive and refreshed every time. To give of yourself, places you amongst the great leaders of history. Jesus, Moses, and Mohammed (peace be upon to them) were all great givers. As long as you keep striving, you will be staying alive.

■ How can this word be applied to your life?

■ How can this word be applied to your family and community?

Keep the faith and keep hope alive.

ALTRUIST

Positive characteristics and traits are valuable possessions. The person who has unselfish qualities will be the one that receives rewards in abundance. Karma is getting what you put out into the universe. Do onto others, as you would want done to you. Sounds familiar? Today is your chance to give someone something that's within your power. It could be opening the door for an elder or telling someone to have a productive day. As long it's sincere, you gave back to the world community. Try it…

■ How can this word be applied to your life?

■ How can this word be applied to your family and community?

Be an altruist type of person; one who is sincerely concerned about the well-being of others.

AMBITIOUS

The go-getter spirit in you is thirsty for the next hurdle to jump over. The ambitious personality that you have within, will take you to the next level of personal success. The weapon of being ambitious blows breath into your dreams and makes them a reality. Russell Simmons is the poster child for being an ambitious person. Become driven and optimistic about challenges that you may come face to face with. Be sure to keep that motivation high, it will lead you to your glory story.

■ How can this word be applied to your life?

■ How can this word be applied to your family and community?

Be ambitious, be a go-getter, and don't stop until you get what's yours in life.

AMEN

Avoid mankind's evil nature. Can I get an "amen" to that? But don't worry; the law of nature 'Opposites' makes sure we have the good with the bad. This means you will want to acquire the positive characteristics of others as much as possible, and refuse the negativity. You can love the people in your life with all that junk, baggage, and moodiness, because their pleasant qualities are just around the corner. But (and I stress BUT) never be afraid to tell them about those ugly and unattractive behaviors that are not bringing them any blessings. You will definitely be doing God's work.

■ How can this word be applied to your life?

■ How can this word be applied to your family and community?

Amen is said after someone speaks music to your heart.

AMUSE

Give a little humor to get a little humor. You want to be happy and have others to share it with, which is a key to building strong relationships. Imagine consistently having happiness induced in your spirit, you will have less dull moments. James Brown sang, "I feel good," and it was very amusing and heartfelt. His rhythm and musical expression was felt by many. Allow your joy to be felt by others, and you will be inducted into the Hall of Fame for your attractive personality.

■ How can this word be applied to your life?

■ How can this word be applied to your family and community?

Amuse the people with your humor and charm.

ANGELIC

To behave in an angelic way, one must display a good-hearted individual. A loving spirit is what draws others to you and your personal life's mission. Your journey towards happiness will attract those that want to experience life in a similar manner. They say, "Birds of the same feather flock together." So, stay in tuned with those whose warm spirit illuminates. That good spirit doesn't chase opportunity away; it increases all chances of obtaining fortune.

■ How can this word be applied to your life?

■ How can this word be applied to your family and community?

Be of good nature and have an angelic spirit.

APPEALING

Your image is very important and never let anyone tell you different. The way you represent yourself to the world should be a top priority. My motto is, "Your appearance says a lot about your self-worth and self-awareness." Also, have an attitude and aura that makes you walk like you are 'big deal'. Bottom line, it begins within and then your dress code puts the icing on the cake. Keep it beautiful inside and out.

■ How can this word be applied to your life?

■ How can this word be applied to your family and community?

Be appealing and watch the positive attention it brings.

APPRECIATE

Once there was a woman who always told her boyfriend, "Thank you very much, I appreciate what you do for me." There was not a time that went by that she didn't give a grand appreciation speech about a gift or some sort of assistance he gave. The boyfriend said, "You don't need to say you appreciate what I do for you all the time, because I know you do." The girlfriend responded, "I'm afraid if I stop saying it, you might stop with the gifts." So, reinforce good attitudes and behaviors in others. Tell family members that you appreciate them, and watch them continue to be a part of your support system.

■ How can this word be applied to your life?

■ How can this word be applied to your family and community?

Appreciate the smallest things people give you,
because no owes you anything.

APPROACH

It is very important how you approach any given situation. There are different levels of energies that may are required for various circumstances. For example: If you are talking to someone of authority, your energy should not be the same as if you are talking to your friends. Your manner should be more respectful and mild. The way you approach a new job, should not be the same energy level as you were chilling out on a Sunday morning. Your approach should change, even when you're on the phone. If it's a very important phone call, you should stand-up, get into a serious zone and deliver your words effectively. It's your approach that counts.

■ How can this word be applied to your life?

■ How can this word be applied to your family and community?

Approach others in a respectful manner, and guest what you will receive?

APPROVE

At times you may feel as though you are just so fly and everybody should know who you are. That may be true, however the approval of others is what we really seek. Sounds crazy, but how would you ever know that you really looked nice the other day. Someone had to stamp it with approval. It can come in many ways: you may get stares, head nods, thumbs up, and other indications. When you have a great idea to relay, it may sound perfect in your mind, but you need approval that it was communicated properly. If someone says, "I understand," that will express that you were clear and concise. Get approved and give approval, but only when it's truthful. Let the social games begin.

■ How can this word be applied to your life?

■ How can this word be applied to your family and community?

Don't approve of things that you don't truly believe.

ASPIRE

You are what you aspire to be. Aspirations come from a place bigger than a career decision. It does come from a similar place of what you want your occupation to be in life. However, having aspirations turns your motivation up a few notches, which provides you with purpose and direction. You take you everywhere you go, and you are much bigger than a place of employment. You become fueled with vision, insight, and a great amount of willpower. What do you aspire to be in life? Go ahead and aspire to be, before your want to dream expires.

■ How can this word be applied to your life?

■ How can this word be applied to your family and community?

Aspire to be great and push it to the limit.

ASSERT

Be assertive, not aggressive when you're resolving an issue. Once a woman said, "The first person who raises their voice loses the battle." Being assertive is respected. Being aggressive is rebellious. The perception of you by others has to be taken into consideration at times. If they say you are aggressive in your approach, you may have to take it down a bit. Sometimes our intentions don't match the behavior. So, be careful and assert yourself in a proper manner.

■ How can this word be applied to your life?

■ How can this word be applied to your family and community?

When you believe in something,
assert your thoughts with passion.

ASSIST

The greatest contributions you can give to your family are to assist them in their journeys towards greatness. Assisting family members to learn and grow will be a beautiful asset for the home team. That beauty will present itself when you may need a little motivation, and here they come with a positive attitude to get you up and running again. Giving assistance to your love ones will never be in vain because you are doing what's right to improve the solidarity of the relationship. As Spike Lee said, "Do the right thing." Be available for assistance to your family.

■ How can this word be applied to your life?

■ How can this word be applied to your family and community?

Assist others in their journey in order to become a better person.

ATTENTIVE

Pay close attention to your virtues. Patience is a virtue. Honesty is a virtue. Do you have them? Yes, you do have them. How do you know you have them? Because everyone has them, it's just up to the individual to utilize them. Your virtues can be maximized or minimized; the choice is yours. Keep a close eye on your valuable qualities and good nature, for they are your winning tickets.

■ How can this word be applied to your life?

■ How can this word be applied to your family and community?

Be attentive when you are learning things that will enhance your life.

ATTRACT

Attract others that are positive, powerful, and creative like you. You are similar to the earth; you have a very powerful atmosphere around you. Just as the earth protects itself from harm of the environmental dangers, your atmosphere operates in the same way. The atmosphere or image you design for yourself will dictate the level of good in your life. Think about it. What and who are you attracting? Are these people building or destroying what you have in life.

■ How can this word be applied to your life?

■ How can this word be applied to your family and community?

Have a character that attracts other beautiful minds.

AWAKE

Awaken the power within, and never let it rest. Your gifts and abilities will sleep and stay inactive, until you scream out, "Wake up!" If those muscles of determination have not been exercised often, you may have to scream two or three times to get it up and running. This personal wake-up call is for you to cause a disturbance in your spirit that has gotten comfortable doing nothing or just the bare minimum. Some people say, "I'm sick and tired of being sick and tired of losing." Some people may wear a charm to express the need to wake up or to stay awake. Whatever you do to awaken the power within, never let it go asleep again.

■ How can this word be applied to your life?

■ How can this word be applied to your family and community?

To be awake and conscious is to be ready for your grand chance in life.

AWARE

Be aware of the way you express yourself. Be aware of the way you represent yourself to the world. Be aware that the world owes you nothing, and you have to claim your position in life. Be aware that life is what you make it. Be aware that you deserve the best. Be aware that every now and then, you will need to refine, refresh, and sharpen your good habits and behaviors. Are you aware that awareness isn't free? The payment will be discipline.

■ How can this word be applied to your life?

■ How can this word be applied to your family and community?

Having the right kind of knowledge and moving carefully.

BALANCE

A lifestyle balance can be compared to the national food pyramid, which provides instructions to help maintain a good healthy diet. Why do we need a healthy body? Simply put, in order to be physically strong. The same idea applies to your lifestyle. There will need to be a balance, so you can be powerful force in life. This can be obtained by a simple method of balancing your wants and needs. That may not sound easy, but just think of all the 'feel good' things we want as soon we set eyes on them. Sometimes you will have to say, "No, I can't get this right now. I have to take care of my needs first." Adjusting your attitude to function in that way, you are moving towards the four riches: emotional, mental, spiritual, and financial.

■ How can this word be applied to your life?

■ How can this word be applied to your family and community?

Look at life as a balancing act, and you're the great performer.

BEAUTIFUL

A beautiful spirit and character is what our parents hoped for when we were born. And that is what they received. However, that changes as we grow up and get older. Life dishes out its fair share of stress, strife, and major challenges that put a strain on the beautiful spirit that you were born with. But hold on and stay committed to keeping that amazing spirit and character, because it's going to lead you to that unlimited financial highway. Personal development is the most beautiful thing in the world.

■ How can this word be applied to your life?

■ How can this word be applied to your family and community?

You are beautiful. Now walk like it!

BELIEVE

There are going to be times when people may not understand why you won't give up. There will be situations when others look at you with doubt. There may be a period in life when everyone else has thrown in the towel and given up. There will be circumstances where there seem to be no way out, but you will have the courage to believe that victory can be only one decision away. Believe in yourself. Hold on tight.

■ How can this word be applied to your life?

■ How can this word be applied to your family and community?

When you believe in yourself, it's like you're the energizer bunny that keeps going and going and going.

BLESSED

One day my mother told me, "I'm too blessed to be stressed." This was at a time when there were lots of difficulties, and she had many reasons to stress. My mother was at a crucial point in her life, where some decisions needed to be made. The path of self-pity was an option, but what good would is that road? Maybe it would have helped to take her stress and place it into the depression box. My mother instead, took the route of self-motivation, self-reliance, and self-esteem. She began to look at others who were in worst situation than her, and began working with the resources she had available. Finding her strengths was a blessing that benefited the entire family.

■ How can this word be applied to your life?

■ How can this word be applied to your family and community?

Count the many blessings you have in life and stop counting the problems.

BOLD

It takes boldness to express individuality today. Why? Because for some reason we are forced to believe that we should dress the same, listen to the same music, talk the same way, and watch the same television programs. Why? Maybe we feel that it's easier to communicate if we all knew the same things? Think about it, if there were more individuality and diversity, communication would be more stimulating. Why? It would then turn communication into discovering and acquiring knowledge and not just passing on the same information. The mature you will begin to say, "Guess what I found out recently?" Be bold, be different.

■ How can this word be applied to your life?

■ How can this word be applied to your family and community?

Be bold enough to be different.

BOUND

Building and having a strong family takes unlimited effort. It's like a good sports team that's always winning. Some of the qualities of a strong team are: communicating, sacrificing, recognizing strengths, teamwork, exercising patience, respect, and helping each other grow individually. Those same behaviors can be applied at home. Family members will have to sacrifice their immediate wants in order for the team to have what's the need first. Everyone will begin to identify specific capabilities and personality strengths, which can develop into a family that operates more effectively. Your home team will be the best in the league. Practice and keep practicing with your team.

■ How can this word be applied to your life?

■ How can this word be applied to your family and community?

Be bound by your family's mission
and never stop helping them strong.

BRAVE

Shakespeare said, "A coward dies a thousand deaths, and a (brave) soldier dies once." You being a brave person will develop you into someone who doesn't easily give up on life or any of the challenges that's a part of life. It's absurd to quit when there's a problem to be solved. Who said you will always have the answer at your fingertips? Some deep searching may be required for certain goals. You begin to kill your spirit by constantly giving up on life. It will make it hard for you to believe in yourself. Now that's a problem. So do as the song says, "Just walk it out," and time will show you that being brave develops a better person.

■ How can this word be applied to your life?

■ How can this word be applied to your family and community?

Be the brave person that saves the day.

CALM

Stay calm, stay cool, and stay emotionally stable in times of a crisis. There are times in life when you will have to be the calm person. For example: You may enter a chaotic situation unexpectedly, and your best thinking may be needed. Be calm. It could seem to be unrealistic because there is a lot of excitement and your heart starts to beat fast; your hands may even begin to sweat. You begin to look around and everyone else is out of control. You may even feel that it would be normal if you lose control in the midst of the confusion. No! Don't do it. Take a moment and reconsider loosing yourself in the moment. Stay calm and be the person others can rely on in those unique times

■ How can this word be applied to your life?

■ How can this word be applied to your family and community?

Be the calm one when it's most needed.

CARE

Oprah Winfrey said, “Lots of people want to ride with you in the limo, but what you want is someone who will take the bus with you when the limo breaks down.” Having people around who truly care about you is important. It also says a lot about you. It reveals that you know what you deserve in life and who should be considered a love one. The care factor comes from a place deep in the soul and will illuminate once it comes to surface. Pick and choose wisely the kind of people that you shine your light on. And more importantly, watch to see how dim or bright their light of care glows.

■ How can this word be applied to your life?

■ How can this word be applied to your family and community?

You are a person who cares about life.

CERTAIN

Be positively certain that you want to have a lifestyle change. Be 100% sure that you want to live better and have assets such as: a strong family, good friends, a positive attitude, emotional stability, a good spirit, and a bank account full of money. Because if you're definite about this, roll-up your sleeves. There's work to be done and it's on your old ugly ways that you're stuck in. It's time to break those bad, unsuccessful, inhibiting habits that have delayed your transformation. If you are not confident on the road to growth and development, your risks factors of failure becomes greater. So, are you certain about this modification that's needed in your life? Raise your hand if you're sure.

■ How can this word be applied to your life?

■ How can this word be applied to your family and community?

Be certain of the direction in life you want travel go and just do it. Don't look back because it will take your eyes off the road.

CHARITY

It is true that giving is from the heart. When someone reluctantly gives, it's not from the good of the spirit. And it won't add to their happiness department, which is priceless. Most of us on planet earth have in common, the want to have a peace of mind and to be happy. Charity is one of the good ways to jump-start that journey. Charity is an expression of joy. If you give to a charity of your choice, you will be making a deposit into your bank account of self-fulfillment. Give to a charity or your local Goodwill and make the connection that most people desire, happiness. Trust me, it feels good knowing you helped someone.

■ How can this word be applied to your life?

■ How can this word be applied to your family and community?

Every time you give to charity you're setting a stage to becoming a more fulfilled person.

CHARM

Your personality is a part of your appearance, and it should also be tailor-made. Your pleasant character with a nice dose of charm equals social enjoyment. Become that social bug that everyone enjoys, and watch your sphere of influence become greater. People can't help but love someone that is approachable, warm-spirited, pleasing to talk to, and charismatic. So go ahead, charm yourself right into your next power move.

■ How can this word be applied to your life?

■ How can this word be applied to your family and community?

Have the kind of charm that gives you a wonderful first impression.

CHEER

Become a person who cheers and shouts encouragement for those in your life. Having the selfless spirit to be someone's cheerleader helps maintain your personal confidence. Sincerely wanting the best for others, places you in a category of "special people". It's very easy to be so consumed with your own situations, issues, and life's struggles that it can seem impossible to cheer for someone else's success. But yes, it is possible and it will reciprocate. Lastly, the biggest benefit is that you will know how to get yourself up and out of a funky mood.

■ How can this word be applied to your life?

______

______

______

______

______

______

■ How can this word be applied to your family and community?

______

______

______

______

______

______

If you are upset, angry, or not feeling well, it feels good for someone to come and cheer you up into a good mood.

CLEAN

It's that time to cleanse your spirit and mind of all that unnecessary baggage and inhibitors. The thoughts that have kept you stuck, cleanse them. The behaviors that have caused conflict in your life, cleanse them. The attitude that leads to arguments, cleanse it. The people who are no good for you, cleanse them. Those places that lead to negativity, cleanse them. The things that you senselessly desire, cleanse them. Once you wash away the ugliness in your character and spirit, your powers will be waiting right there.

■ How can this word be applied to your life?

■ How can this word be applied to your family and community?

Clean up your act and stop delaying your progress.

CLEAR

There will be times when your actions may not clearly express what your intentions were, and that doesn't feel good. When you have really, really good intentions, it feels even worst. Making your understanding, understood could be a challenging task at times. For example: The person that is receiving your message can flat out perceive it wrong. It may even be the wrong timing. Certain atmospheres can cause a lack of energy and in turn, your words can become unimportant to the receiver. There can be too many people, with too many different insights (that's never fun). You could be unenthusiastic and communicate in a lazy manner. There are many things that can hinder a crystal clear understanding, and cause chaos. So know life is an art, and be very clear when you're painting a masterpiece.

■ How can this word be applied to your life?

■ How can this word be applied to your family and community?

Be clear about the words that come out of your mouth, because they can either hurt or help your progress.

COMFORT

So what your past life hasn't been that great. If you used drugs in the past, that's fine. You're overcoming a health problem; that's fine, too. You've had self-esteem issues before, that's not a problem. You were a habitual relationship destroyer, that's fine. Your life has been filled with major challenges, which is fine. Why is everything fine? Because once you take a vow to become a different person and make the correct steps to right those wrongs, your resurrection will begin. Repeat the following phrase every time you feel you don't deserve to be golden. "I was blind, but now I see." You were blinded by circumstances and a lack of motivation. But now your eyes are wide open reading this information. This means, you're now responsible for taking action. Gotcha!

■ How can this word be applied to your life?

■ How can this word be applied to your family and community?

Make today, the day you begin being totally comfortable with your past mistakes.

COMMEND

There are times when you may want to let others know they're doing a good job. That's nice. But right now, take the time to commend yourself for jumping through the fire hoops of reaching accomplishments and enduring trials and tribulations. Life hasn't been a big sweet piece of cake. You have taken the roses with the thorns; the challenges of success and failure, and you have been there still hopeful. This is why you should take the time and pat yourself on the back. Give credit where credit is due. You have been living life and karate chopping those issues, problems, and struggles. So now, take a good look in the mirror and be proud of yourself.

■ How can this word be applied to your life?

■ How can this word be applied to your family and community?

You should commend yourself for having the courage for seeking out ways to become a better person. Negativity is so easily obtainable; go for the challenge of being productive.

COMMIT

If you are committed and keep your promises in a relationship with a love one, there's a big chance it's going to be a successful relationship. The same applies to your personal growth and development. If there's a goal you have and you really want it, stay committed and keep the promises you made to yourself. There will be strong results. Becoming a committed person is like going to the gym and getting muscles. You have to work out and you will become stronger. The small things that you committed yourself to, adds to the muscle tone in your character. Every time you commit to something, you're working those muscles and strengthening your personality. Eventually you are going to have a habit of being committed. That's a pretty good habit to have.

■ How can this word be applied to your life?

■ How can this word be applied to your family and community?

What will it take for you to reach your goals and big dreams? Commit yourself to them, and you'll see.

COMPASSION

Compassion is the humane quality of understanding the suffering of others and wanting to do something about it. Have you ever felt that way? It's a deep human connection. Most of the time we communicate on the surface and most daily activities only require a simple level of human relations. The infamous surface is as normal as saying "good morning". It can become a regular way to function. To get to your compassionate side more often, you may have to break the so-called norms. The next time someone says, "Good morning", stop them and shake their hand, look them in the eyes and say, "How are you? How's everything?" Be interested in others. Don't be so surface all the time; it can become a bad habit. Bring out your compassion to others, but don't forget to use it with CAUTION.

■ How can this word be applied to your life?

■ How can this word be applied to your family and community?

Having compassion is listening with care, in order to respond with concern.

COMPOSE

Without order, there is chaos. Your life deserves structure and you can arrange or rearrange all the needed changes. The choice is yours. Let's take a look at society, for example: Imagine if there were no laws, structure, traffic lights, street signs, speed limits, DWI laws, or all that helps maintain order. It would be hell on earth. The same concept applies to building or rebuilding structure in your life. If there is none, it will be like a nightmare. Without life management, you are relying on luck only. Some say, "If I'm lucky, things will make sense in my life." That's not a responsible way to bring about change and structure. There will need to be a more proactive approach, not a head lost in the clouds way of living. Begin composing, strategizing, organizing, and coordinating your future.

■ How can this word be applied to your life?

■ How can this word be applied to your family and community?

Be the greatest composer in your life and harmoniously fine-tune yourself into success.

CONCERN

Pay close attention to the behaviors being presented in your relationships. Don't be a couch potato and just watch your relationships have no quality or high definition (HD). Don't be a lazy communicator. Be totally involved in how it functions. For example: One day I said to a potential friend, "You always get overexcited and agitated when there's an issue to be solved. I don't like that and I can't get used to that." He responded, "You are right, and I kind of allowed it to become a part of me." I then said, "I noticed a lot of people around you tolerate it, like it's just who you are. It concerned me because I would like for us to keep hanging out with each other. But maybe now is not the right time." That was a time in my life when I was cleaning out my closet and letting go of a lot of unnecessary junk. I was then and still am very concerned about the people I give a VIP pass to my life.

■ How can this word be applied to your life?

■ How can this word be applied to your family and community?

Be genuinely concerned about the relationships in your life.

CONFIDENT

If you don't believe in yourself, who else should? The way of the world today, no one has the time or patience to tolerate a person with low self-confidence. That's unfortunate, but honest. Having a lack of confidence gets in the way and slows down productivity. If you're in a relationship and the other person has to be your personal motivational coach 75% of the time, there will be no room for relationship stuff and it's not fair. Now as for 'work force' America, a low level of confidence can be viewed as a lack of ability to make decisions and function effectively at work. You don't want to mess with your bread and butter (money). So to keep your confidence department healthy, here's a tip: When things don't go right, don't sweat the small stuff. Take it as a training course in, "I know what to do next time."

■ How can this word be applied to your life?

■ How can this word be applied to your family and community?

Your confidence level is one of the key components in your road to riches: emotionally, spiritually, and financially

CONFIRM

We, the people, are walking feelings and emotions. All interactions we have with each other have an F&E (feelings and emotions) base. This is the reason why the need to confirm your dedication and commitment to others is highly important. When someone says, "Get back to me and let me know what you're going to do about what we discussed." It doesn't matter how important you may view the person. A piece of their heart and trust is within that statement. Expecting you to live-up to a verbal agreement is a very simple civil obligation. Imagine if you expected someone to let you know if they were going to be in your wedding, and they never responded. Ouch, that hurts. To keep the people in your life from having a possible heart attack from stress, confirm your position on the subject or issue that's on the table. A clear yes or no will do. Believe me, you will sleep better at night.

■ How can this word be applied to your life?

■ How can this word be applied to your family and community?

Confirm and affirm your loyalty at home, work, or at school.

CONSCIENCE

Some may have a misunderstanding that to be a conscience person, you have to be a Mr. or Mrs. Know it all. No one will ever know it all. If you decide to make the wise choice to be a conscious person, you will focus on things you want to be informed about. If you want to know about Global Warming, get up to date information on it. If you have a desire to be knowledgeable about politics, Google it. Maybe you really have an interest in flying airplanes; go to the local library. You have the right to consciously and individually choose your interest. Being conscious is thinking big.

■ How can this word be applied to your life?

■ How can this word be applied to your family and community?

Being conscious means you are not sleepwalking.

CONSIDER

Simply consider that people deserve a basic level of respect. Once you make that consideration, your travels in life will become more pleasant and less difficult. Be mindful of what you say to others, in hopes that you don't hurt their feelings. Consider making another's experience comfortable when possible. When these and other considerations are made for the common good, you have chosen to live through positive lenses in life. This will give you a sense of confidence, and it won't be so easy for someone to break your spirit. Consider being high off of life with a positive attitude, and just watch the way people begin responding to your aura. Some may not know how to handle you being so graceful.

■ How can this word be applied to your life?

____

____

____

____

____

____

■ How can this word be applied to your family and community?

____

____

____

____

____

____

You should consider making it your business to be respectful to others.

CONSOLE

To console is to be there through tough times. My mother says, "Everybody needs somebody." Having the ability to console someone, says that you are an asset to loved ones. The idea of having a healthy and good spirit is very important in the act of consoling someone. You will have to become open and feel free to express even those hidden bones (secrets), if they can help someone at that time. When consoling others to a healthy emotional state, you will have to be sincere in your efforts. So work on maintaining a good spirit, just in case you are called to help a broken soul.

■ How can this word be applied to your life?

____

____

____

____

____

____

■ How can this word be applied to your family and community?

____

____

____

____

____

____

Reconfirm to your love one's know everything will be alright, and that time usually reveals change.

CONTENT

It is wise to never overlook your blessing or the accomplishments you've made, thus far in life. When you have the ability to find happiness in who you are and what you have, the possibilities to become a greater person is highly obtainable. All goals may not be realized to their fullest extent, but why not find glory in what you have achieved? Did you know that being content could be utilized in becoming proactive? Accepting and being responsible for where you are in life, is the first step towards developing a better you. Now move on full steam.

■ How can this word be applied to your life?

■ How can this word be applied to your family and community?

Be content, not complacent.

COURAGE

The power within is realized when you have the courage to use your abilities to reach the next plateau in life. Courage is in you, sitting and waiting for its chance to grow into a powerful force. How will it grow? By facing your fears. For example: A firefighter that has to go into a burning building (they're human too) to save a child. A family member of that child is screaming, "I want to go and get my love one!" The firefighter then gets the concerned person removed from the scene and says, "I'll go." That is courage wanting to become a stronger force by continuously facing fears. A firefighter has to stay courageous, in order to get the job done. And you will also have to become and stay courageous, in order to save your life and all those aspirations you have. Courage is a winning habit that will keep you successful.

■ How can this word be applied to your life?

■ How can this word be applied to your family and community?

Courage exits only in the face of fear.

CREATIVE

Producing creative thoughts takes some sacrifice and patience. You will need to be open-minded. Passion will need to be in existence. Persistence is a main ingredient. A nice amount of courage will be good too. Thinking outside the box will be a nice addition. You can't forget about the motivation; it's the heartbeat. Oh yes, self-esteem keeps everything valuable. Synergize when the time is right. A small pinch of stubbornness; too much is not good though. And with all this mixed into a big pot, you will have creative juices overflowing. Your creative mind will be ready to become a contributor to society.

■ How can this word be applied to your life?

■ How can this word be applied to your family and community?

Creative people are those that dare to be.

DEDICATE

Strong results are the consequences of being dedicated. The story about how a slow turtle won the race against a fast-running rabbit is a story of dedication. You would think that a turtle couldn't outrun a rabbit. However, it was the dedication of the turtle that made the impossible, possible. The rabbit on the other hand, entered the race choosing to not be dedicated. Instead, the rabbit was blinded by arrogance. He felt that no matter what, a turtle could never beat him racing. So during the race, he ate food and took a nap. He definitely disregarded the abilities of his opponent, which is always a mistake. The turtle was slowly moving forward with dedication and won the race. Constant movement and dedication are the ingredients that will keep you winning. K.I.M. (Keep It Moving).

■ How can this word be applied to your life?

■ How can this word be applied to your family and community?

You are either dedicated or not; there is no in between.

DETERMINED

Ask yourself, why should I be determined to be successful and happy in life? Whatever your answer was, there needs to be a good reason to be determined. Your motive should be clear and concise. When you think about what motivates you to be determined, it should play out like a movie. You have to seriously feel it, taste it, and see yourself in action. Always know that there are millions of people with hopes and dreams, but a small percentage hold on tightly to the reasons that fuel determination. Failure waits until you run out of gas. Be grounded in your reasons to stay determined.

■ How can this word be applied to your life?

■ How can this word be applied to your family and community?

Have a good reason to be determined and your goals will stay alive.

DILIGENT

There was a girl who was diligent and victorious throughout her life. Her name was Charlene. She was born in the inner city with many difficulties. But Charlene worked diligently not to be a victim of circumstances. In high school, she was involved in as many extra-curriculum activities as she could handle. Charlene knew she did not want to be deterred from her goals. Her diligence was strong. Then when she got to college, Charlene retraced of all her winning habits diligently. Then with diligence she graduated from that Ivy League University. Finally, the president of the United States hired her, and those diligent behaviors were at it again. She did it, and you can do it too. Be diligent.

■ How can this word be applied to your life?

■ How can this word be applied to your family and community?

Success is the fruit, and diligence is a perfect seed to plant.

EDUCATE

Be a knowledge seeker and you will be taking responsibility for educating yourself. Once upon a time, there was an old wise man whose knowledge flowed like a river. On a day like this one, a young fellow said, "I would like to receive great information in order to be knowledgeable." The wise man said, "Meet me out in the fields later today and I will provide you with some." The young man went to fields, but there was no one there. He tried it the next day, and still, the elder never showed. He wanted to educate himself, but there was always a no show from the old wise one. Until one day, the young man respectfully approached the wise man and said, "Why are you not coming as you promised?" The clever and smart man replied, "I was waiting on you to come find me. So please don't be upset. Here's the information you wanted. I just wanted you to see, how much you were willing to seek knowledge."

■ How can this word be applied to your life?

■ How can this word be applied to your family and community?

Education is revealed every time you open your mouth.

ENERGETIC

Be happy to be alive. Be excited about your future. Be overzealous about the loved ones in your life and highly appreciate them. Feel elated about your last accomplishment, because it could have been a failure. You should be ecstatic that life has made you a stronger person, by learning from your mistakes. Are you extremely happy that you woke up this morning? Well act like it, and get your energy up to par, now! Be energetic in your interaction with others. Go ahead and be a walking energy drink.

■ How can this word be applied to your life?

■ How can this word be applied to your family and community?

Be energetic in your efforts to organize your life.

FAITH

Faith is like a sword in combat. Some say it's the breath that keeps you alive. My mother told me faith is the devil slayer, which sounds kind of scary. A gentleman told me that when people get married, they should close their eyes for at least the first five years. Now that's having faith. However viewed, it's there for you when needed. And once you've become a friend to it, you can begin advocating its beauty. You will be able to give stories about your missions that were life threatening, and how faith rescued the voyage. We have to give faith its props. It's a big deal.

■ How can this word be applied to your life?

■ How can this word be applied to your family and community?

No one owns faith; it's utilized as needed.

FOCUS

It is better to be focused on success, instead of just watching others obtain it. Choosing to remain a focused person, will help you fight off negativity without even raising a finger. The focus factor comes alive when there are very important things that have to get done, and forces a clear runway. Even though, in the past we've all gotten lazy and kind of sat back and let things just happen. Today is a new day and you know you are responsible for your success. Being and staying focused is the best way to approach your goals and aspirations. Take the advice of a multi-millionaire like Jay-Z who said, "FOCUS MANNN!"

■ How can this word be applied to your life?

■ How can this word be applied to your family and community?

If you look into a focused person's eyes, you might see lasers.

FREE

Financial freedom is the American dream. Have the ability to go on vacations whenever and wherever your heart desires. Have the money to buy that dream home without worrying about the price tag. Finally purchase the car you always wanted, with all cash and no payments. Having a walk-in closet filled with all your favorite shoes and designer clothes. Being able to be a philanthropist and contribute financially to a good cause. This kind of good living comes with a big price tag of its own, and it's called responsibility and more responsibilities. It was said that everything that glitters isn't gold. So go ahead and make it a goal to be financially free, but just know that you will be a very busy person with mountains of obligations. It won't be all fun and games. But it's well worth the effort.

■ How can this word be applied to your life?

■ How can this word be applied to your family and community?

Imagine being financially able to buy whatever you need and want in life.

GIFT

You can look at giving a gift as anticipatory joy. That feels so good. For example: Think about the time you've bought a gift for a love one. First you are hit with the nice and special reason to purchase it, which feels good. Maybe they accomplished something or made it through the storms of challenges. Next, you begin to decide what to buy them and what they might like. The good thought of the person's character appears in your mind. Then, the decision-making process between the final two special gifts has to be made. Both gifts are very nice, but you feel you need to get the perfect one. The choice was made and you got the present that is just right and will compliment them. Finally, you begin to prepare and set up a time to meet. Once you come face to face and hand over the present, you almost express more joy than the receiver of the gift. They have a big smile and you a bigger one. It's a valuable and healthy human experience every step of the way. Give a gift.

■ How can this word be applied to your life?

■ How can this word be applied to your family and community?

Your duty for today will be to give a gift to a loved one.

GIVE

Do you want to be someone who makes a contribution to the world? Then you will be in the category with greats such as: George Washington Carver, who invented peanut butter; Garrett Morgan, the person responsible for supplying the U.S army with its first gas masks; or Mae C. Jemison, the first African-American woman in space. Imagine giving yourself to the world in such a way. That won't be a problem, and I have the perfect place for you to start. Did you know that you can give your good spirit to people and it will have a great impact? Yes, your spirit. In fact, you will become responsible for DEVELOPING positive atmospheres all across the globe. You will be the one that is HONORED for turning negative situations and finding a positive. You will make a great CONTRIBUTION to an organization, once the people see your bright and shining character. The world will be blessed to have you as a giver.

■ How can this word be applied to your life?

■ How can this word be applied to your family and community?

Give your good nature to others and you will be contributing to society.

GLORY

When we think of giving glory, it's usually for someone other than ourselves. Not today. Because you are going to find glory in whom you are and where you've come from. I met someone years ago, and they were ready to discredit all that had made them who they were. The person expressed to me that his past life was filled with negativity, wrong doings, frustration, self-hatred, bad attitude, foul mouth, and other disturbing things. At that time, this individual was making some progress in turning their life around, which was progress. He had low self-esteem, which caused his growth process to become a dubious task. I expressed to him that he's trapped in self-defeating thoughts and is blocking his development. He looked at me as if he needed more clarity. I looked him dead in his eyes and simply said, "Be happy that you made it this far, and use all that strength that got you here, to keep going." While staring in the sky, he said, "I did come a long way." Never throw yourself away, there's some good stuff in there.

■ How can this word be applied to your life?

■ How can this word be applied to your family and community?

Have glory in the success of your day.

GOALS

First and foremost, don't be afraid to set goals. It can carry a little fear of the 'what ifs'. But on the other hand, 'what if' you don't set goals or have plans? I think that's a lot more reckless. The biggest mistake people make is they feel that a goal is not a goal, unless it's the million dollar one. The big ones... In turn, they end up setting fewer goals and begin to lack the skills to set them effectively. There are short-term goals and long-term goals that can keep you busy setting them. Short-term goals are hourly, daily, weekly, and up to 6 months. Long-term goals are 7 months and better. The secret to accomplishing those big goals is to go after the small ones first.

■ How can this word be applied to your life?

____

____

____

____

____

____

■ How can this word be applied to your family and community?

____

____

____

____

____

____

If there are no goals, there's no direction in your life. You do understand that right?

GROW

Rap superstar Nas has a song on his Stillmatic album titled "2nd Childhood". This song talks about how some people don't want to grow up. As time moves, you will be smart to mature with it. As you mature there will be growing pains, which at times may have a person wanting to escape and be a kid again. I can relate to that. But you can't feel that way all the time, that'll be a big problem. In your growth as a human being you will have ups, downs, good and bad times, relationships fallouts, new people, sickness and health, and all the other things you've experienced so far. However you look at it, you're on an ongoing training course. And I know you are ready to continue the process of growth and development. Particularly because you were once in your mother's stomach, kicking and showing signs that you were ready to come out and grow up. So I know you are not breaking your birth agreement.

■ How can this word be applied to your life?

■ How can this word be applied to your family and community?

Some people grow physically, but choose to be stuck mentally.

GOD

There is a story about a man and his unfortunate misunderstanding of God. It was the day before Thanksgiving and there was a terrible fire at this apartment building. All of the children and adults made it out safely, except this man named Mr. Unaware. He was trapped at the top of the burning building, screaming for his life. The Fire Department was called and they immediately sent a fireman up with a ladder. The fireman said, "Ok buddy, slowly grab my hand and we will be on the ground in no time." Mr. Unaware responded, "I'm not going anywhere; I'm waiting on my God." The fireman pulled the ladder down and minutes later, another one was sent up the burning building. This fireman said, "Now you listen to me. Get on this ladder; the building is about to burn down." Mr. Unaware screamed back, "No, I am waiting on my God!" The ladder went down with the fireman and so did the building. The moral of the story is that God sends blessings in many ways, and you have to be aware and recognize them. God doesn't always package your blessings exactly the way you imagined. Open your eyes and look at all God's blessing.

■ How can this word be applied to your life?

■ How can this word be applied to your family and community?

There are times in life when Divine Intervention is what's needed to bring back the order in your life.

HOPE

The foundation of hope is a positive attitude. Thinking and feeling good about life helps propel hope. Having an open mind allows hope to be easily accessible. The idea of having hope can be tied to your trust department. This is the reason most people say, "Hope for the best, but expect the worst." We have been lied to, let down, and mislead a few times in life, which slowly closes the doors of trust. However, today is the day that your future is depending on you to revitalize hope and bring trust back into existence. A slow process is still a process, and any effort beats no effort. You are going to have to come in from the dead of hopelessness, and begin trusting your decisions. Hope and be responsible, they work well together.

■ How can this word be applied to your life?

■ How can this word be applied to your family and community?

Hope for the best and prepare for new adventures.

HUMANE

One thing for sure and two things for certain, humankind is interdependently connected. Long ago, there was a humanitarian song called, "We Are the World." This song expressed that the suffering around the world belongs to all mankind. International and national issues involving inhumane treatment of people are a humanity problem. But if sheltered and wealthy parts of society disregard other societies' pains, it shall be in their backyards one day. Recently there was a tragedy by the name of Hurricane Katrina. The pain of those who suffered could not be disregarded. It took the efforts of people from many nationalities to assist, which was humanely ethical. It felt right to help. The innate spirit of people is to be humane. Don't give up on what's natural.

■ How can this word be applied to your life?

■ How can this word be applied to your family and community?

All humans were created to live together in harmony.

HUMOR

It is said that humor is good warm soup for the soul. A broken spirit is so common that there should be emergency humor boxes throughout cities (Pull In Case Of Emergency). There have been times I've given love ones perfectly wrapped gifts, and they were surprised with a joke book. After a while, I stopped being amazed that people were so happy and excited to receive such a gift. Mainly because there are times a person may need a little pick-me-up laughter, when no ones around. Another good reason to a have some humor in your character, is because one day you might be the only doctor in the room to help heal a broken heart. Put humor in your life and smile.

■ How can this word be applied to your life?

■ How can this word be applied to your family and community?

Give a little humor as a form of a good daily deed.

IMAGE

A Sprite soda slogan is, "Thirst is everything. Image is nothing." Hopefully too many people didn't take that seriously. Your image is everything, and I need to really stress that point. If you knew that already, take it as a reminder. If you didn't know, now you are responsible. There are two types of images you want to keep polished. First, it's your dress code. Not how expensive your clothes are, but your standard for representing yourself has to be considered. Your dress code is the first of the two, because of the communication called body language. People see you first. Being approachable is important to the empire you are building. You never know if you will bump into Oprah; please look like you can represent her company if hired. Last, but certainly not least, the image of your attitude is very important. It is highly suggested that you imprint a positive image in people's head, so they will remember the next great entrepreneur, politician, doctor, CEO, manager, lawyer, teacher, or real estate mogul. Let your presence be felt, and keep both images positively ready for the opportunity of your life.

■ How can this word be applied to your life?

■ How can this word be applied to your family and community?

Your image is a key component in your road to success.

IMPROVE

What does it take to improve your life, or to take it to the next level? First let's start with critical self-evaluation. That has the ability to provide you with data about your strengths and weaknesses. It also keeps you in touch with the reality that you are not perfect, and there is always room for improvement. The second suggestion to improve your life is to have a strong willingness to take what you've evaluated and make some goals. You will need to be enthusiastically ready mentally and emotionally, in your path to victory. Your determination has to become your cheerleader on the sideline screaming, "YOU CAN DO IT!" Finally, it's time for some action. You have those lasers in your eyes and it's on now. Nothing can stop you from improving your life… nothing!

■ How can this word be applied to your life?

■ How can this word be applied to your family and community?

There is always room for improvement.

INTELLIGENT

"I" over "E" meaning Intelligence over Emotions, is a method to help a person function socially effectively. This technique can be utilized to keep you out of many emotion wars and all that comes with that territory. Your intelligence is there to manage your emotional state before it totally controls your behaviors. When your emotions have all the power over a situation, your intelligence takes a back seat and goes to sleep for a few minutes. Falling asleep behind the wheel is dangerous. You become a mess when your emotions erupt. The consequences of your emotional riot are not measured when your intelligence doesn't step in to play mediator. You don't want to be someone who reacts emotionally all the time; instead, your proactive thinking will keep you an effective individual. Next time you feel like reacting, just repeat, "I over E, I over E. Intelligence over Emotions"

■ How can this word be applied to your life?

■ How can this word be applied to your family and community?

Your intelligence is going to keep you together emotionally.

INTEREST

When you become interested in something, it's like a spark that starts a fire. Sometimes it happens unexpectedly, and it's like a new found friend. Also, there are times where you may want to search for a new interest. A spanking new interest can breathe life into your daily routine. Once that blood starts pumping and excitement is running through your veins, it spreads throughout your life's activities. You will begin to put more efforts into your relationships, work, or school. The feel good hormones will pour out of your heart and into everything you touch. Now, do you think it's time to find a new interesting activity? Go ahead and treat yourself to life. Don't cheat yourself.

■ How can this word be applied to your life?

■ How can this word be applied to your family and community?

When you are interested in something,
make a transition into it becoming a part of your life.

KNOWLEDGE

Knowledge is the foundation of your life. Knowledge is obtained through all five of your senses: sight, hearing, touch, taste, and smell. You gain respect through your knowledge box; please know that. The people in your life are connected through the commonality of knowledge or interests you all share. Your job or school requires your best knowledge. Knowledge has a lot to do with your current position in life, whether you're winning or losing, weak or powerful. Knowledge is everywhere. Look around you. But be careful with the kind of knowledge you allow to be a part of your life. Screen the knowledge and see if it's worthy enough for you to believe in. Everything is not for everybody. Have an idea of the kind of knowledge you want, and the kind that doesn't even fit who you are.

■ How can this word be applied to your life?

■ How can this word be applied to your family and community?

Knowledge gives birth to wisdom and understanding.

LOVE

Love is an action word. It represents what you do in a relationship. Janet Jackson said in her song, "What have you done for me lately?" The words "I love you" are nice, but to show love is much more pleasing to the feelings department. To love is to sacrifice and be patient. Those are major action words. Sacrificing your wants for the betterment of the love, you will have to stop being stubborn, selfish, and closed-minded. Having patience for love, means you can't be a quitter, easily aggravated, or a bad listener. Love can be too much for the average slackers, because they don't have enough energy to fulfill the basics. A woman once told me that a person would be lucky to have one true friend. But once that love one arrives, remember to do the running-man dance, sacrifice, and be patient. Stay actively involved in your relationships

■ How can this word be applied to your life?

■ How can this word be applied to your family and community?

Make a vow to be a friend and love one for better or for worst.

MATURE

There are cycles in life that we all experience. Each cycle has its appropriate time limit. We are first a baby with very limited control. The psychologist Sigmund Freud said that by the age of five we have a character, which is progress in the developmental process. The adolescent stage is where we learn a lot about the body and hormones. The teenager is ready for maturity, but is not sure if he or she wants to give up the freedom of doing foolish things at times. Now you move up to the age of twenty-one, which is pretty much the last year of stupid excuses. Finally, adulthood is the place where there are little or no excuses for having immature behaviors. There is definitely zero tolerance for an immature adult. So with all that said, mature people come in all ages, colors, shapes, and sizes. Be mature, it fits you.

■ How can this word be applied to your life?

■ How can this word be applied to your family and community?

Maturity is when you stop behaving like a child.

MODEL

We, the people, are all followers. However, it is what you follow that is of concern. That is the reason your individuality is important as the protector of self-identity. Yes, you will like and appreciate qualities or styles in another person. Yes, you may want to try out the latest trend; that's ok. The importance of not becoming 'molded like clay' is what you want to avoid. You don't want to slowly kill off your natural self, totally. A make-over is needed at times, but never become a clone. The power of your individuality will give you the liberty to agree or disagree with things that come your way. Individuality expresses your will to be capable of modeling behind things that fit like a glove into your personality...not just any old thing.

■ How can this word be applied to your life?

■ How can this word be applied to your family and community?

Be sure to model behind winning behaviors.

MORAL

You were born a moral person, untouched and sheltered from negativity. Then moral values were also taught at an early age through simple instructions such as: never give up, listen to your elders, don't tell fibs, and don't touch fire, because you can get burned. There have been years of basic directions of how to be a positive-thinking person. However, it's the challenge of preserving the good that's within, due to all the negativity and immoral behaviors that are ready to invite your participation. Through effective methods of refining your morals, you will keep your spirit warm and will keep yourself in a place of good nature. Read spiritually uplifting materials and have relationships with those who want to maintain a positive lifestyle.

- How can this word be applied to your life?

- How can this word be applied to your family and community?

Your moral department is what makes you do the respectable things in life.

MOTIVATE

There will be many times you will need to motivate yourself through the rough roads leading to success and happiness. Self-motivation is like a mechanism inside of you with an on and off switch. The thing about this mechanism is that you will want to leave it on more than having it turned off. Because the constant use of motivation develops into a positive habit. It will be like having a superpower. For example: Farrah Gray, the author of Reallionaire, was raised in Chicago surrounded by a poor quality of life. However, he kept his switch of motivation on, and he made his first million at the age of 14. He expressed that poverty was his motivation to become successful. Can you imagine how people were reacting to such a powerful entrepreneur at that age? They were probably asking, "What is he motivated by?" Motivation and you, is a very personal relationship. Get to know it.

■ How can this word be applied to your life?

■ How can this word be applied to your family and community?

Motivation is the super fuel that keeps your desires and goals moving.

PATIENCE

When was the last time you displayed patience? Was steam coming out of your ears? Patience can be very difficult to give at times, especially when you don't receive it that often. Almost everywhere you go; patient people are absent when you need them. You can be at work, in a supermarket line, or just sitting in traffic. All this negative energy enters your spirit, and it can be difficult for you to exercise patience. It's like you've been zapped so many times throughout the day, that you want to zap someone. But hold on to your good nature. You are having a nice day and you can't let anyone take your joy. Don't give impatient people the power over you.

■ How can this word be applied to your life?

■ How can this word be applied to your family and community?

Patience is a virtue, when you decide to use it.

PEACE

The search for peace is something that all people have on their agenda. The level of importance for peace is different from person to person. It may be at the top of your list and nearly at the bottom for the next person. However, the fact remains that peace is a precious gem. A wise old woman once said, "You will never know how valuable peace is, until you step out of the madness." When a hostile environment surrounds you, you find a way to function. If you are stuck in a traffic jam and the horns are blowing, and people are screaming at each other, you get through the craziness. When life seems to keep putting up roadblocks, you operate in the strife. But once you get your hands on some peace, life becomes beautiful all over again. A nice hot aromatherapy bath, the smell of some fresh cut flowers, the setting of the sun, or snuggling under a warm blanket are some of the ways to get back to a peaceful state of mind.

■ How can this word be applied to your life?

■ How can this word be applied to your family and community?

Chaos is due to absence of peace.

POWER

How do you know if you have the power? The way people respond to you is a big indicator. The knowledge that you have acquired through so many different ways, are the source of where your power comes from. If you have been indulging in things that have no strength, your actions will be weak. Every time you have a superficial hour-long conversation, your relationships will deteriorate. When you give up easily in times of struggle, your decision-making skills become fragile. But as a person, who wants to be powerful, begin to be more conscious of who and what you believe in. Your power can be found in your belief-system.

■ How can this word be applied to your life?

■ How can this word be applied to your family and community?

Spark the power within!

PREPARE

Life has no guarantees and you will always be involved in risks. Preparing for life's challenges lessens the risk factors of disappointment. Of course failures come with success, and you shouldn't fear the possibility of coming up short at times. However, there is something called *The Stages of Change,* which is a system that can assist in obtaining your aspirations. It starts with your desire to change, which a motivating factor that will energize the want to become a more powerful person. Preparation, your next most important step, is to strategically devise short and long term goals. Then you will take those well-prepared plans into the stage of action. Your desires and hopes will then begin to materialize. Lastly, you will then monitor your progress.

■ How can this word be applied to your life?

■ How can this word be applied to your family and community?

Prepare properly, and your performance will make you proud.

POSITIVE

Choosing to be a positive person in a world where negativity can be at your doorstep, requires some real discipline. However, being positive will prevail. The energy impresses others to want to join forces with your movement of good behaviors. The exciting energy that comes with being a positive person is a form of stimulation. This strength that comes from being a positive person, keeps you bright and shining in the face of difficulty. Your positive attitude gives you the power to seek the light in the darkness of a situation. It gives you open-mindedness and creativity. Having a positive outlook on life is just more beneficial than being a negative person.

■ How can this word be applied to your life?

■ How can this word be applied to your family and community?

Being a positive person will express the power of choice. You can be a negative person, but not today

PUPPET

Who or what is pulling your strings? Is it materialism, low self-esteem, diets, fantasy, media, or a desire to be accepted? There are many things that can cause your life to become unmanageable. There are two areas that can bring the Puppet alive in your life: the war within or the war of social pressures. Both aspects can be definitely linked to your emotions. This is why the need for self-evaluation is very important, in order to recognize the rise of the Puppet within. You don't want it to grow out of control. Here are the 3W's of self-evaluation to prevent unmanageability in your life:

1) What are my strengths and weaknesses? [This will create a stronger you.]
2) When are the times that I'm most vulnerable to my negative urges? [This will help monitor your bad habits.]
3) Why do I need to evaluate my life? [This will restart the evaluation process.]

■ How can this word be applied to your life?

■ How can this word be applied to your family and community?

Your bad habits can delay your transformation.

PURPOSE

Having a purpose in life, gives you a reason to be excited about the future. It provides support for the well-being of your spirit. The down side of life caused by rejection, losses, and disappointment, can be heavy on the heart and spirit. The dire need to be successful and happy can keep you going head to head with challenges that may result unfavorably at times. However, having that purpose branded on your soul, plays as a covenant, protecting you emotionally on your travels through the storms. I encourage you to make a purpose or mission statement, as a reminder of who you are on this planet. For example: My purpose in life is to help others. Keep the statement simple.

■ How can this word be applied to your life?

■ How can this word be applied to your family and community?

What is your present purpose in life?

RESPECT

In a relationship, respect is expected. It's a normal practice. But when it comes to self-respect, the high expectations should stay the same. There should be an impressively grand level of respect you have for yourself. People can see that level of respect you have for yourself, through your strut or swagger. Self-respect causes you to make mature decisions that you can be proud of. The decision not to use drugs is respectful. The decision not to violate others is respectful. The decision to honor family members is respectful. Everybody is always talking about respect, whether having it and giving it. Why? You can think about that, and then discuss it with your love ones. That should be good respectable conversation.

■ How can this word be applied to your life?

■ How can this word be applied to your family and community?

Respect yourself and others will benefit greatly.

STRIVE

As your life's journey continues, never forget to use the abundance of power that you have within. Strive to achieve. Strive for advancement. Strive to be alive. Strive to be angelic. Strive to be appealing. Strive for your aspirations. Strive to assist others. Strive to be aware. Strive to have balance. Strive to be beautiful. Strive to be charitable. Strive to be charming. Strive to be committed. Strive to be confident. Strive to be conscious. Strive to have courage. Strive to be creative. Strive to be dedicated. Strive to be diligent. Strive to be disciplined. Strive to be distinguished. Strive to be effective. Strive to have empathy. Strive for excellence.

■ How can this word be applied to your life?

■ How can this word be applied to your family and community?

You can't stop and you won't stop. You are going to the top!

I would like to end the book with a poem by my son Tyrone S. Hartman (19 yrs old). The chance for me to include him on anything I do is a pleasure. The process of assisting family members to grow and feel alive is everyone's obligation. I appreciate my son's energy and motivation to be great. Keep up the good work. His poem is below:

What She Is To Me

What she is to me,
she is a person who is with you no matter what.
What she is to me,
she is someone special that you
can tell your dreams and fears.
What she is to me,
she is a person that loves you for who you are.
What she is to me,
she is a lady that you can spend
the rest of your life with.
What she is to me,
she is someone that I can never seem to find.

The End

TO CONTACT THE AUTHOR

Walk Into Your Destiny Media

Author: **Tyrone Hartman**

walkintodestiny@yahoo.com
or
973-392-7299